DIANA PALMER

A MAN OF MEANS

D0126938

Published by Silhouette Books
America's Publisher of Contemporary Romance

SILHOUETTE BOOKS

ISBN 0-373-76429-4

A MAN OF MEANS

Copyright © 2002 by Diana Palmer

Visit Silhouette at www.eHarlequin.com

Printed in U.S.A.

Books by Diana Palmer

For Cissy at Writerspace, Sara, Jill and Celeste, and all the wonderful readers, many of whom I was privileged to meet in Atlanta in 2001 at our author tea, who visit me online there at my Web site. Love you all. DP

One

Meredith Johns glanced around her worriedly at the out-of-control Halloween party-goers in their colorful costumes. Meredith was wearing an outfit left over from college days. She made a good salary at her job, but there was no money for little luxuries like Halloween costumes. She had to budget just to be able to pay the utility bill in the house she shared with her father.

The past few months had been traumatic, and the wear was telling on her. She needed to get out of the house, Jill, one of her colleagues, had said firmly—especially after her most agonizing experience at home. Meredith was reluctant. Her father was only just back at their house after three days. But Jill was insistent. So she'd put on the only costume she had, a bad choice in many ways, and walked the three blocks to her friend's downtown apartment. She grimaced at her surroundings. What an idiot she'd been to come to this wild party.

But it really had been a tumultuous week for Meredith

and she'd wanted to get her mind off her troubles. Her father's violent behavior at the house they shared was unnerving. They were both still grieving, but her father had taken the tragedy much harder. He felt responsible. That was why a scholarly, conservative college professor had suddenly retired from his job and turned into an alcoholic. Meredith had tried everything she could think of to get him into treatment, but he refused to go on his own accord and the treatment facilities which would have taken him wouldn't unless he went voluntarily. Only a violent episode that had landed him in jail had temporarily spared her of this saddening experience. But he was out three days later and he had a new bottle of whiskey. She still had to go home after the party. He'd warned her not to be late. Not that she ever was.

Her grey eyes were sad as she sipped her soft drink. She had no head for alcohol, and she was as out of place here as a cup of tea. Not only that, her costume was drawing unwanted attention from the men. So was her long blond hair. It had been a bad costume choice, but it was the only thing she had to wear on the spur of the moment. Going to a Halloween party in her street clothes would have made her stand out, too.

She moved away from a slightly tipsy colleague who wanted to show her around Jill's bedroom and unobtrusively put her glass on a table. She found Jill, pleaded a headache, thanked her for a "good" time and headed out the front door as fast as she could. Once on the sidewalk, she drew in a long, sweet breath of fresh air.

What a bunch of wild people! She coughed delicately, remembering the unmistakable smell of that smoke that had been thick enough to obstruct clear vision inside. She'd thought it would be fun to go to a party. She might even meet a man who would be willing to take her out and cope with her father. And cows might fly, she told herself. She hadn't been out on a date in months. She'd invited one prospective date to her home for supper. But after a good look at her father, who was mean when he drank, the prospective suitor took off. Her heart wasn't in it, anyway. Recently she'd given up trying to attract anyone. She had her hands full already. Her grief was still fresh, too.

An odd noise attracted her attention as she started back toward her own house. She felt self-conscious in her getup, and remembering the lewd remarks she'd drawn from a man who was normally very polite and gentlemanly, she was sorry she hadn't had a coat to wear. Her clothes were mostly old, because by the time she made the mortgage payment and took care of the bills, there wasn't much left over. Her father couldn't work and wouldn't get help, and she loved him too much to desert him. It was becoming a costly proposition.

She wrapped her arms around herself and hoped she was covering up enough skin to discourage stalkers. But her skirt was very short and tight, and she was wearing fishnet hose, very high heels, a low-cut blouse and a flaming pink feather boa. Her blond hair was loose around her shoulders and she was wearing enough makeup to do justice to a ballet recital. She winced, hoping she hadn't been noticed. She'd gone to the party as a burlesque dancer. Sadly she looked more like a professional hooker in her garb.

She rounded a corner and saw two shadowy figures bending over what looked like a man on the ground.

"Hey! What do you think you're doing there?!" she yelled, making as much noise as possible. Then she started running toward them and waving her arms, yelling threats as she went.

As she expected, the surprise of her aggressive presence shocked them into retreat. They jumped up and ran away, without even looking back. The best defense, she thought with faint amusement, was always a good offense. It was a calculated bluff, but she'd seen it work for women smaller in stature than she was.

She ran to the downed man and examined him the best she could in the dim glow of the streetlights.

Concussion, she thought, feeling his head and encountering a metallic smelling wetness. Blood. He'd been hit on the head by his assailants, and probably robbed as well. She felt around under the jacket he was wearing and her hand touched something small and square on his belt. She pulled it out.

"Aha," she said with a triumphant grin. A man dressed as well as he was could be expected to have a cell phone. She dialed 911 and gave the operator her location and the condition of her patient, staying on the line while the dispatcher got an ambulance en route.

While she waited for it, she sat down on the pavement beside the man and held his hand.

He groaned and tried to move.

"Don't do that," she said firmly. "You'll be okay. You mustn't move until the EMTs get here. I haven't got anything to treat you with."

"Head...hurts."

"I imagine it does. You've got a heck of a bump. Just lie still. Feel sick, sleepy...?"

"Sick," he managed weakly.

"Lie still." She lifted her head to listen for the ambulance, and sure enough, a siren sounded nearby. The hospital was less than two blocks from her home, maybe four from here. Lucky for this guy, whoever he was. Head injuries could be fatal.

"My...brothers," the man was whispering brokenly. "Hart...Ranch. Jacobsville, Texas."

"I'll make sure they're contacted," she promised.

He gripped her hand, hard, as he fought not to lose consciousness. "Don't...leave me," he ground out.

"I won't. I promise."

"Angel," he whispered. He took a long, shaky breath,

and went back into the oblivion he'd left so briefly. That wasn't a good sign.

The ambulance rounded the corner, and the headlights spilled out onto Meredith and her patient. She got to her feet as two EMTs, one male and one female, piled out the doors and rushed to the downed man.

"Head wound," she told them. "Pulse is slow, but steady. He's coherent, some nausea, his skin is cold and clammy. Blunt force trauma, probably mild concussion..."

"Don't I know you?" the female EMT asked. Her face brightened. "Got you! You're Johns!"

"That's me," Meredith said with a grin. "I must be famous!"

"Sorry, not you—your dad." She winced at the look on Meredith's face.

Meredith sighed. "Yes, he spends a lot of time on ambulances these days."

"What happened here?" the woman asked quickly, changing the subject. "Did you see anything?"

"I yelled and scared off two guys who were bending over him," she volunteered. "I don't know if they were the ones who hit him or not. What do you think?" she added as the woman gave him a professional once-over.

"Concussion, definitely," she agreed. "Nothing broken, but he's got a lump the size of the national debt here on his head. We'll transport him. Coming along?"

"I guess I should," Meredith said, waiting until they loaded him onto the gurney. He was still unconscious. "But I'm not exactly dressed for visiting a hospital."

The EMT gave her a speaking glance. "Should I ask why you're dressed like that? And does your boss know you're moonlighting?" she added wickedly.

"Jill Baxley had a Halloween party. She thought I should come."

The other woman's eyebrows levered up. "Jill's parties

are notorious for getting out of control. I've never even seen you take a drink.''

''My father drinks enough for both of us,'' came the reply. ''I don't drink or use drugs, and I need my head examined for going to that party. I escaped early, which is how I found this guy.''

''Lucky for him,'' the woman murmured as they loaded him into the back of the ambulance. ''Judging by his condition, he could have died if he hadn't been found in time.''

Meredith climbed up into the back and sat down on the bench while the driver got in under the wheel and the female EMT called the hospital emergency room for orders. It was going to be a long night, Meredith thought worriedly, and her father was going to be very upset when she got home. He and her mother had been really close, but her mother had been fond of going to parties and staying out until the early morning; sometimes with other men. Recent events had made him dwell on that behavior. Her father seemed to have transferred that old contempt to her. It made her uneasy to think of arriving home in the wee hours. Anything could happen. On the other hand, how could she leave this man? She was the only person who knew who to contact for him. She'd promised to stay with him. She couldn't let him down.

He was examined by the resident on duty in the emergency room, who diagnosed concussion. He'd been unconscious most of the way to the hospital, but he'd come out of it just once to look up at Meredith and smile, tightening his big hand around the fingers that were holding it.

His family had to be notified, and Meredith was coaxed into making the call to Jacobsville for the harassed and overworked emergency room staff.

She was given a phone and a telephone directory which also listed Jacobs County, of which Jacobsville was the county seat. She looked through it until she found a listing for Hart Ranch Properties, Inc. That had to be it.

She dialed the number and waited. A deep, drawling voice answered, "Hart Ranch."

"Uh, I'm calling for a Mr. Leo Hart," she said, having found his driver's license in the wallet his assailants hadn't had time to steal. "He's at Houston General…"

"What happened?" the voice asked impatiently. "Is he all right?"

"He was mugged. He has a concussion," she added. "He can't give the staff any medical information…"

"Who are you?"

"I'm Meredith Johns. I work…"

"Who found him?"

"I did, actually. I called the ambulance on his cell phone. He said to call his brothers and he told me where they were…"

"It's two o'clock in the morning!" the voice pointed out angrily.

"Yes, I am aware of that," she began. "It only happened a little while ago. I was walking down the street when I saw him on the sidewalk. He needs his family—"

"I'm his brother, Rey. I'll be there in thirty minutes."

"Sir, it's a long way to Houston from where you are. If you drive that fast…!" she said at once.

"We have an airplane. I'll get the pilot out of bed right now. Thanks." He added that last word as if it hurt him, and hung up.

Meredith went back to the waiting room. Ten minutes later, she was admitted to the room where the victim had been examined.

"He's conscious," the attending physician told her. "I'm going to admit him overnight, just to be sure. Any luck with his family?"

"His brother is on the way, in his own plane, apparently," she said. "I didn't get a thing out of him. Sorry."

"People get upset and they don't think," the resident said with a weary smile. "How about staying with him? We're understaffed because of that respiratory virus that's going around, and he shouldn't be alone."

"I'll stay," she said with a grin. "It's not as if I have a hectic social life."

The resident pursed his lips and smirked at her outfit.

"Halloween party," she said, grimacing. "And next time I get invited, I'll have a broken leg, I swear it!"

Forty-five minutes later, there was a problem. It was six feet tall, had black hair and dark eyes and it erupted into the hospital cubicle like an F-5 tornado, dressed in jeans and boots and a fringed rawhide jacket thrown carelessly over what looked like a beige silk shirt. The wide-brimmed hat slanted over those threatening eyes was a Stetson, one of the most expensive made, with its distinctive feathered logo pin on the hatband. He looked impressively rich, and excessively angry.

The man was livid when he saw his big brother, still drifting in and out of consciousness, on the examining table. He gave Meredith a scrutiny that could have peeled paint off old furniture, his eyes narrowing contemptuously on her costume.

"Well, that explains why you were on the street at two in the morning," he snarled angrily. "What happened? Did you feel guilty and call for help after you tried to roll him?" he added sarcastically.

"Look here," she began, rising.

"Save it." He turned to the big man on the table and laid a lean, strong hand on his brother's broad chest. "Leo. Leo, it's Rey! Can you hear me?" he asked in a tone that combined affection with concern.

The big man's eyes blinked and opened. He stared blankly up at the leaner man. "Rey?"

"What happened to you?" Rey Hart demanded gently.

Leo grinned wearily. "I was thinking about new forage grasses and wasn't paying attention to my surroundings," he murmured drowsily. "Something hit me in the head and I went down like a brick. Didn't see a thing." He winced and felt clumsily in his pockets. "Damn! My wallet's gone. So's my cell phone."

Meredith started to tell him that she had the phone and wallet in her purse for safekeeping, but before she could speak, Rey Hart gave her a furious, speaking glance and walked out of the cubicle like a man hunting a fight.

His brother drifted off again. Meredith stood beside him, wondering what to do. Five minutes later, Rey Hart walked back in accompanied by a tall man in a police uniform. He looked familiar, but Meredith couldn't quite place him. She knew she'd seen him before.

"That's her," Rey told the policeman, indicating Meredith. "I'll sign anything necessary as soon as I see that my brother's going to be okay. But get her out of here."

"Don't worry. I'll handle it," the policeman said quietly. He handcuffed Meredith with easy efficiency and pulled her out of the cubicle before she could protest.

"I'm being arrested?" she exclaimed, stunned. "But, why? I haven't done anything!"

"Yes, I know, I've heard it all before," the officer told her in a bored tone when she tried to explain what had happened. "Nobody's ever guilty. Honest to God, dressed like that, out on the streets alone after midnight, you were bound to be up to no good. What did you do with his cell phone and his wallet?"

"They're in my pocketbook," she began.

He confiscated it from her shoulder and propelled her out of the building. "You're going to be in a lot of trouble. You picked the wrong man to rob."

"See here, I didn't mug him! It was two men. I didn't see their faces, but they were bending over him as I came down the sidewalk."

"Soliciting is a felony," he pointed out.

"I wasn't soliciting anything! I'd just come from a Halloween party dressed as a burlesque dancer!" she raged, furious that she was being punished for having done someone a good turn. She read his name tag. "Officer Sanders, you have to believe me!"

He didn't say a word. He drew her with him, firmly but gently, and put her into the back seat of the police car.

"Wait," she told him before he could close the door. "You get my wallet out of my purse and look in it. Right now," she insisted.

He gave her an impatient look, but he did what she asked. He looked through the plastic inserts in her wallet and glanced at her with a changed expression. "I thought you looked familiar, Johns," he murmured, using her last name, as most people she knew at work did.

"I didn't mug Mr. Hart," she continued. "And I can prove where I was when he was being mugged." She gave him her friend Jill's address.

He gave in. He drove to Jill's apartment, went to the door, spoke to an obviously intoxicated and amused Jill, and came back to the squad car. He let Meredith out of the back of the squad car and took off the handcuffs. It was cool in the night air, and Meredith felt self-conscious and uncomfortable in her garb, even though the police officer knew the truth now.

"I'm really sorry," he told her with a grimace as he met her grey eyes. "I didn't recognize you. All I knew was what Mr. Hart told me, and he was too upset to think straight. You have to admit, you don't look very professional tonight."

"I do realize that. Mr. Hart cares about his brother, and he doesn't know what happened," she pointed out. "He walked in and saw his brother on the table and me dressed like this," she indicated her clothing, "and his brother said his wallet and cell phone were missing. He doesn't know me from a stump. You can't blame him for thinking the worst. But those two men who hit him would have gotten his wallet if I hadn't come along, and they're still on the loose.''

"Can you show me where you found him?" he asked.

"Of course. It was just down the sidewalk, that way."

She led and he followed her, with his big wide-angle flashlight sweeping the sidewalk and the grass as they walked. She pointed to an area of flattened grass. He left her on the sidewalk and gave the area a thorough scrutiny, looking for clues. He found a candy wrapper and a cigarette butt.

"I don't guess you know if Mr. Hart smokes or likes candy?" he asked.

She shook her head. "Sorry. All he told me was his brothers' name and where they lived. I don't know anything more about him.''

He stood up. "I'll ask his brother later. Wait here while I call for one of the technicians to bag this evidence," he told her.

"Okay," she said agreeably, drawing the feather boa closer. It was getting cold standing around briefly clad, waiting for crime scene investigators. "Somebody's going to love being turned out of bed to come look at a cigarette butt and a candy wrapper," she stated with helpless amusement.

"You'd be surprised at what excites those guys," he chuckled. "Catching crooks isn't exactly a chore to them. It's high drama.''

"I hope they catch these two," she said firmly. "Nobody should have to be afraid to walk down the streets at night. Even after dark, dressed like this, alone," she added pointedly, indicating her clothes.

"Good point," he was fair enough to admit.

He called in his location and requested crime scene technicians. Meredith was ready to go home, but she couldn't

leave until she'd given the policeman a statement for his
report. She sat in his car, with the overhead lights on, writing out what she knew of the attack on Leo Hart. It didn't
take long, because she didn't know much.

She handed it back to him. "Can I go home now?" she
asked. "I live with my father and he's going to be upset
because I'm coming home so late. I can walk. It's only
about three blocks from here."

He frowned. "Your father is Alan Johns, isn't he?" he
asked. His expression changed. "Do you want me to go
with you?"

She didn't usually flinch at facing her irate parent. She
was gutsy, and she could handle herself. But tonight, she'd
been through a lot. "Would you?" she asked, uneasy because her fear was visible.

"No problem. Get in."

He drove her to her house and went to the door with her.
The house was dark and there was no movement inside.
She let out a sigh of relief. "It's okay. If he was awake,
the lights would be on. Thanks, anyway," she said with a
smile.

"If you need us, call," he said. "I'm afraid I'll be in
touch again about this. Rey Hart already reminded me that
his brother is our state attorney general. He's not going to
let this case go until it's solved."

"I don't blame him. Those guys are a menace and
they're probably still running around looking for easy targets to rob. Take care."

"You, too. And I'm sorry about the handcuffs," he
added, with the first smile she'd seen on his lean face since
her ordeal began.

She smiled back. "My fault, for wearing a costume like
this on the streets," she admitted. "I won't do it again.
Thanks for the ride."

Back at the hospital, Rey Hart sat by his brother's bed-
side until dawn, in the private room he'd obtained for him.

He was worried. Leo was the hardiest one of the lot, and the most cautious as a rule. He was the prankster, always playing jokes, cheering them up in bad times. Now, he lay still and quiet and Rey realized how much his sibling meant to him.

It infuriated him that that woman had thought nothing of robbing his brother while he was sick and weak and helpless. He wondered what she'd hit him with. She wasn't a big woman. Odd, that she'd been able to reach as high as Leo's head with some blunt object. He recalled with distaste the way she'd been dressed. He was no prude, but in his early twenties he'd had a fling with a woman he later found out was a private call girl. He'd been infatuated with her, and thought she loved him. When he learned her profession and that she'd recognized him at once and knew how wealthy he was, it had soured him on women. Like his married brothers had been, and Leo still was, he was wary of females. If he could find a man who could bake biscuits, he told himself, he'd never let even an old woman into the house ever again.

He recalled their latest acquisition with sorrow. He and Leo had found a retired pastry chef who'd moved in with them—the last of the Hart bachelors—to bake their beloved biscuits. She'd become ill and they'd rushed to the drugstore to get her prescriptions, along with candy and chocolates and a bundle of flowers. But her condition had worsened and she'd told them, sadly, that the job was just too much in her frail state of health. She had to quit. It was going to be hard to replace her. There weren't a lot of people who wanted to live on an isolated ranch and bake biscuits at all hours of the day and night. Even want ads with offers of a princely salary hadn't attracted anyone just yet. It was depressing; like having Leo lying there under white sheets, so still and quiet in that faded striped hospital gown.

Rey dozed for a few hours in the deep night, used to sleeping in all sorts of odd positions and places. Cattle ranchers could sleep in the saddle when they had to, he thought amusedly, especially when calving was underway or there was a storm or they were cutting out and branding calves and doing inventory of the various herds.

But he came awake quickly when Sanders, the police officer who'd arrested that woman last night, came into the room with a murmured apology.

"I'm just going off shift," Officer Sanders told Rey. "I thought I'd stop by and tell you that we've gone over the scene of the attack and we have some trace evidence. The detectives will start looking for other witnesses this morning. We'll get the people responsible for the attack on your brother."

Rey frowned. "Get 'them?'" he queried. "You've already got her. You arrested her!"

Officer Sanders averted his eyes. "Had to turn her loose," he said uneasily. "She had an alibi, which was confirmed. She gave me a statement and I took her home."

Rey stood up, unfolding his intimidating length, and glared at the officer. "You let her go," he said coldly. "Where's my brother's cell phone?" he added as an afterthought.

The policeman grimaced. "In her purse, along with his wallet," he said apologetically. "I forgot to ask her for them when I left. Tell you what, I'll swing by her house and get them on my way home…"

"I'll go with you," he said curtly. "I still think she's guilty. She's probably in cahoots with the guys who attacked Leo. And she could have paid someone to lie and give her an alibi."

"She's not that sort of woman," the policeman began.

Rey cut him off angrily. "I don't want to hear another word about her! Let's go," he said, grabbing his hat, with a last, worried glance at his sleeping brother. He wondered how the policeman could make such a statement about a woman he'd just met, but he didn't really care. He wanted her in jail.

He drove his rental car, with the off-duty policeman beside him, to Meredith's home, following the directions Officer Sanders gave him. It was in a run-down neighborhood, and the house was in poor condition. It only intensified Rey's suspicions about her. She was obviously poor. What better way to get money than to rob somebody?

He went to the door, accompanied by the policeman, and knocked. Hard.

He had to do it three times, each with more force and impatience, before someone answered the door.

Meredith Johns was disheveled and white-faced. She was clutching a bulky washcloth to her face and wearing a robe over the clothes she'd had on the night before.

"What do you want now?" she asked huskily, her voice slurred and jerky.

"Been drinking, have you?" Rey Hart asked in a blistering tone.

She flinched.

Officer Sanders knew what was going on. He read the situation immediately. He stepped past Rey, grim and silent, grimacing when he saw Meredith's face. He went by her and into the living room and began looking around.

"Hard night, I gather? It must be a continual risk, in your profession," Rey said insinuatingly, with a speaking glance at her dress in the opening of the old, worn robe. "Do your marks make a habit of beating you up?" he added with cold contempt.

She didn't answer him. It was hard to talk and her face hurt.

Officer Sanders had gone into the bedroom. He came back two minutes later with a tall, disheveled but oddly dignified-looking man in handcuffs. The man, who'd been quiet before, was now cursing furiously, accusing Meredith of everything from prostitution to murder in a voice that rose until he was yelling. Rey Hart looked at him with obvious surprise. His eyes went to Meredith Johns, who was stiff as a poker and wincing every time the man yelled at her. The policeman picked up the telephone and called for a squad car.

"Please, don't," Meredith pleaded, still clutching the ice-filled cloth to her face. "He's only just got out..."

"He isn't staying. This time, he's going to be in jail for longer than three days," the officer said firmly. "You get to the hospital and let one of the residents look at you, Miss Johns. How bad is it? Come on, show me," he demanded, moving closer.

Rey stood by, silent and confused, watching as Meredith winced and moved the bulky cloth away from her face. His breath was audible when he saw the swelling and the growing purple and violet discoloration around her eye, cheek and jaw.

"God Almighty," Rey said harshly. "What did he hit you with?"

"His fist," the policeman replied coldly. "And it isn't the first time. You have to face facts, Miss Johns," he told her. "He isn't the man he used to be. When he drinks, he doesn't know what he's doing. He'll kill you one night when he's like this, and he won't even remember doing it!"

"I won't press charges," she said miserably. "How can I? He's my father! He's the only family I have left in the world...."

The policeman looked at her with compassion. "You don't have to press charges," he told her. "I'll provide them myself. You'd better phone your boss and tell him you won't be in for a few weeks. He'll have kittens if you walk into the office looking like that."

"I suppose he would." Tears ran down her pale cheeks,

all the more eloquent for being silent. She looked at her raging, cursing father and sadness claimed her features. "He wasn't like this before, honest he wasn't," she told them. "He was a kind, loving, caring man."

"Not anymore," Officer Sanders replied grimly. "Get to the hospital and have your face seen about, Miss Johns. I'll take your father outside until the unit comes…"

"No," she groaned. "Please, spare us that! I can't bear to have the whole neighborhood watching, hearing him…like that, again!"

He hesitated. "Okay. I'll watch for them out the window. The unit can drop you by the hospital, since it's going there first…."

"I'll take her," Rey said at once, without wondering why he should do such an about-face. He didn't trust the woman, or even totally believe her story. But she did look so pitiful. He couldn't bear to leave her in that condition to get to the hospital. Besides, whatever her motives, she had gotten help for Leo. He could have died if he hadn't been cared for.

"But…" she began.

"If," he added coldly, "you change clothes first. I am *not* being seen in public with you in that rig!"

Two

Meredith wished she felt up to a fight. Her long blond hair was down in her face, her grey eyes were sparking fire. But she was sick to her stomach and bruised. She would rather have gone to bed if these stubborn men would just have let her alone. But her face could have broken or shattered bones. She knew that. She grimaced, hoping her insurance would cover a second "accident" in as many months.

When the unit arrived, Meredith turned away from the sight of her raging father being carried off and closed the door. Probably it wasn't surprising to the neighbors anymore, it happened so often. But she hated having everyone know.

"I'll get dressed," she said in a subdued tone.

Rey watched her go and then shoved his hands into his pockets and looked around the room. It was shabby. The only bright things in it were books—hundreds of them, in bookcases and boxes and stacked on tables and chairs. Odd, he thought. They were apparently short of cash, judging by the worn old furniture and bare floor. There was only a very small television and a portable stereo. He glanced at the CD case and was surprised to find classical music dominating the discs. What a peculiar family. Why have so many books and so little else? He wondered where the woman's mother was. Had she left the father, and was that why he drank? It would have explained a lot. He knew about missing parents, especially missing mothers—his had left the family while the five Hart boys were young, without a backward glance.

Minutes later, Meredith came back, and except for the bruised face, he might not have recognized her. She was wearing a beige sweater set, with a tweed coat over it. Her blond hair was in a neat bun and her face devoid of makeup. She wore flat-heeled shoes and carried a purse that looked new.

"Here's your brother's cell phone and his wallet," she said, handing it to him. "I forgot to give them to Officer Sanders."

He glared at them and put them in his pocket. He wondered if she'd have given them back at all if he hadn't come here. He didn't trust her, regardless of what the policeman had said. "Let's go," he said stiffly. "The car's outside."

She hesitated, but only for a minute. She wasn't going to be able to avoid a checkup. She knew the problems that negligence could cause. Even a relatively minor problem could become major.

Unexpectedly Rey opened the car door for her. She slid in, surprised to find herself in a new luxury car. She fastened her seat belt. His brother, Simon Hart, was state attorney general. Rey owned a ranch. She remembered how his injured brother, Leo, had been dressed last night, and her eyes went to Rey's expensive hat and boots and silk shirt. Of course, they were a wealthy family. Considering her state of dress—or undress—the night before, she could understand his misgivings about her character.

She sat wearily beside him, the ice-filled cloth still in her hand. She held it to the side of her face that was bruised and hoped that it would spare her some of the swelling. She didn't need a doctor to tell her that it was a bad blow. The pain was almost unbearable.

"I took a hit to the face a few years ago in a brawl," he volunteered in his deep, slow drawl. "It hurt like hell. I imagine your face does, too."

She swallowed, touched by the faint concern. Tears threatened, but she never cried now. It was a weakness she couldn't afford.

He glanced at her, puzzled. "Nothing to say?"

She managed to get her voice under control. "Thank you for taking me to the hospital," she said huskily.

"Do you usually dress like that when you go out at night?" he asked belatedly.

"I told you. There was…a Halloween party," she said. It hurt to talk. "It was the only costume I had."

"Do you like parties?" he asked sarcastically.

"My first one…in almost four years," she managed to say. "Please…hurts…to talk."

He glanced at her and then was quiet. He didn't like her. He didn't trust her. Why was he taking care of her? There was something unexpectedly vulnerable about her. But she had spirit.

He walked her into the emergency room. She filled out forms and was ushered back into a treatment cubicle while Rey sat in the waiting room between a squalling toddler and a man coughing his head off. He wasn't used to illness. He'd never seen much of it, and he didn't know how to cope with it. Accidents, sure, he was a good hand in an emergency, and there were plenty on a ranch. But he hated hospitals.

Meredith came back a good thirty minutes later with a prescription and a frown.

"What did he say?" he asked conversationally.

She shrugged. "He gave me something…for pain," she said, waving the prescription.

"They sent me to a plastic surgeon," he volunteered as they went through the automatic door.

She didn't speak.

"I had a shattered bone in my cheek that they couldn't repair," he persisted.

"I'm not…going…to any damned…plastic surgeon!"

His eyebrows arched. "Your face could be distorted."

"So what?" she muttered, wincing because it really did hurt to speak. "It's not…much of a face, anyway."

He scowled. She wasn't pretty, but her face had attractive features. Her nose was straight and elegant, she had high cheekbones. Her mouth was like a little bow, perfect. Her eyes, big and grey, fascinated him.

"You should go," he said.

She ignored him. "Can you…drive me by the pharmacy?"

"Sure."

She gave him directions and he waited while she had the prescription filled. He drove her back to her house and left her there reluctantly.

"I'll be at the hospital with Leo if you need anything," he said as if it pained him to say it.

"I don't need any help. Thanks," she added stiffly.

His eyebrows arched. "You remind me of me," he murmured, and a thin smile touched his lips—a kind one. "Proud as Lucifer."

"I get by. I really am…sorry about your brother. Will he be all right?" she asked at her door.

He nodded. "They want to keep him for two or three days. He'll want to thank you."

"No need. I would have done it for anyone."

He sighed. She was going to look bad for a long time, with her face in that condition. She'd been beaten and he felt responsible, God knew why. He took a breath. "I'm sorry I had you arrested," he said reluctantly.

She pursed her lips. "I'll bet...that hurt."

"What?"

"You don't apologize much, do you?" she asked, as if she knew.

He scowled down at her, puzzled.

She turned away. "No sweat. I'll live. So long."

She went in and closed the door. Rey, who'd done without companionship for a number of years, suddenly felt alone. He didn't like the feeling, so he shoved it out of his mind and drove back to the hospital. He wouldn't see her again, anyway.

Leo came back to himself with a vengeance late that afternoon. He had Rey lever the head of his bed up and he ate dinner with pure enjoyment.

"It's not bad," Leo murmured between mouthfuls. "But I wish I had a biscuit."

"Me, too," Rey said on a sigh. "I guess we could buy a restaurant, as a last resort," he added dejectedly. "One that serves breakfast."

"Who was that woman who came in with me?" he asked Rey.

"You remember her?" Rey was surprised.

"She looked like an angel," he mused, smiling. "Blond and big-eyed and all heart. She held my hand and sat down on the sidewalk in the cold and talked to me until the ambulance got there."

"You were unconscious."

"Not all the time. She even came in with me on the ambulance," he said. "She kept telling me I was going to be all right. I remember her voice." He smiled. "Her name was Meredith."

Rey's heart jumped. He felt uneasy. Leo usually didn't

pay much attention to strange women. "Meredith Johns," he agreed.

"Is she married?" Leo asked at once.

Rey felt threatened; it irritated him. "I don't know," he said.

"Do you think you could find somebody who knows how to get in touch with her?" his brother persisted. "I want to thank her for saving me."

Rey got up from the chair where he'd been sitting and walked to the darkened window, peering out through the blinds while he played for time. "She lives near the place where you were attacked," he said finally, unable to lie.

"What does she do for a living?"

"I don't know," Rey said, feeling uncomfortable. He couldn't get her father's accusing remarks out of his mind. She'd said she was dressed up for a party, she'd even found someone to give her an alibi, but Rey didn't completely believe her. What if that whole defense was a lie? What if she was some sort of prostitute? He didn't want his brother getting mixed up with a woman like that. He didn't trust women, especially strange women. Then he remembered her poor, bruised face and he felt bad about his suspicions.

"I'll ask one of the nurses," Leo said abruptly.

"No need," Rey told him. He turned back around with his hands in his pockets. "If you're determined, I'll go get her in the morning and bring her in to see you."

"Why not tonight?"

Rey let out an impatient breath. "Her father roughed her up because she got home late last night. I took her to the emergency room this morning before I came back here."

Leo's eyes narrowed and went cold. "Her father beat her? And you took her back home to him?" he said angrily.

"He wasn't there. They took him off to jail," he said. His face hardened even more. "She'll have a hell of a bruise. They said she couldn't go back to work for a few weeks." He moved one shoulder restlessly. "Considering the way they live, I don't know how she'll manage," he added reluctantly. "They don't seem to have much. Apparently the old man doesn't work and she's the only one bringing home any money." He didn't volunteer his opinion of how she made it.

Leo leaned back against the pillows. His big frame was without its usual vibrance. His dark eyes were dull, and his lean face was drawn. His blond-streaked brown hair was unkempt, and looked odd in the back where they'd had to shave it to put stitches in. It was a reminder of how tricky head wounds were. Leo was very lucky not to have brain damage. Rey thought about the assailants and his eyes blazed.

"I'm going to phone Simon tonight," he told Leo. "I'm sure the local police will do all they can to catch the guys who waylaid you, but they'll work even harder if they get a call from the state attorney general."

"There you go again, pulling strings," Leo mused.

"It's for a good cause."

"Did you find my wallet and my cell phone?" Leo asked.

"The woman had them. They're in my pocket."

"Good. I didn't think she had anything to do with mugging me. Don't forget your promise to bring Meredith here in the morning," he said.

Now it was "Meredith." Rey didn't like the whole idea of having Leo around the woman, but he didn't have a legitimate reason for keeping her from Leo's side. It would sound even more suspicious if Rey started throwing out sarcastic remarks about her. Leo did love to pull his chain.

"Okay," he said reluctantly.

"Good man," Leo replied with a wan grin. "Nothing like family to look after you."

"Next time, watch your back instead of daydreaming about forage grasses," Rey said firmly. Then he leaned

forward in the chair. "So, tell me what sort of grasses the
Cattleman's Association is advocating."

Rey got a hotel room near the hospital, so that he could
have a bath and get some rest. The night staff had the phone
number, so they could call him immediately if he was
needed.

He phoned Simon before he went to bed.

"Leo's been mugged?" Simon exclaimed. "And you
didn't call me last night?"

That tone was still intimidating, even though Rey was
thirty-one. Simon was the eldest of the five brothers, and
the bossiest, next to Cag.

"I was too upset to phone anybody," Rey returned, "and
too busy trying to handle...another problem that cropped
up. He's all right. Honest. I didn't find out until the early
hours of the morning, and it's been a long day. He was
already out of danger before it occurred to me that I needed
to let you know."

"All right," Simon said, sounding as if he was more
relaxed. "Do they have a suspect?"

"No. I thought we did, but it turned out to be a dead
end," he added, without going into details about Meredith
Johns. "There were two of them, and they haven't been
caught. It's a miracle he wasn't killed, and that they were
stopped in time before they robbed him. You might give
the local police chief a call. Just to let him know we're all
interested in solving the case."

"You want me to use my influence for personal gain?"
Simon drawled.

"Hell, yes, I do!" Rey shot back. "This is our brother,
for God's sake! If a big, strong man like Leo can get
mugged in a residential neighborhood, so can anybody else!
It doesn't say a lot for the security in this area."

"No, it doesn't," Simon agreed. "I'll point that out to
the police commissioner, first thing tomorrow. Then I'll run

down to Jacobsville and get Cag and Corrigan and we'll be right up to see about Leo.''

Rey chuckled. It was the first bit of humor he'd felt so far. The five brothers rarely went so far as to gang up on people, but considering the size and reputation of them, they got results when they did. This was an emergency, anyway. They could have lost a brother. The perpetrators had to be caught.

"They should be home by now," Rey replied. "I couldn't phone them because they were showing those Japanese businessmen around the ranch and the town."

"I'll see how much luck they had. Japan is very careful about its import beef. The fact that we run organically raised cattle will certainly go in our favor," Simon said.

"Yes, it will. Get some sleep. And don't worry about Leo. He's fine. I'd never have left the hospital if I'd had one doubt about that."

"I'll stop worrying."

"Give my love to Tira and the boys," Rey added.

"I'll do that. See you tomorrow."

Rey hung up, thinking about Simon and his family. Tira was redheaded and gorgeous, and the boys favored both of them, although they had Simon's dark eyes and hair. Corrigan and Dorie had a boy and a girl. Cag and Tess had just a boy, but they were talking about how nice a daughter would be. Meanwhile, Rey and Leo enjoyed being uncles, but had no interest in joining the ranks of the married.

If it wasn't for those biscuits, Rey thought miserably. It was going to be expensive to have the local café make biscuits for them every day until they employed a new biscuit maker, but if they got desperate enough, and offered enough of an incentive, they could probably manage it.

Turning his attention elsewhere, Rey gave a thought to poor Leo with his stitches and his headache, and another to Meredith Johns's bruised face. Tomorrow, he'd have to deal with Leo's request to see her, and he wasn't looking forward to it. He wished he knew why.

Rey went to Meredith Johns's house the next morning after he'd had breakfast. It took her a minute or two to answer the door, and for an instant, he thought that perhaps she might not be in any condition to answer it. She'd been badly bruised.

But she opened the door and peered up at him bravely, even though she looked like a refugee from a bar brawl. Her left eye was swollen shut completely now.

"Leo wants to see you," he said easily, noticing how the top of her blond head only came to his shoulder. She wasn't tall. Even bruised, her face had a beautiful complexion. Her mouth was pretty. He shook himself mentally. "He wants to thank you for what you did. He remembers that you rode in on the ambulance with him. You didn't tell me that," he added with faint accusation.

"I wasn't thinking," she said. "I was worried about what would happen when I came home late."

"Have you heard any more about your father this morning?" he asked grimly.

"They're going to charge him with simple battery," she said heavily. "I can't afford a lawyer. He'll have a public defender and he'll probably have to stay in jail for a few weeks." She looked up at him. "It will be a godsend, you know, because he'll dry out completely."

He hated the compassion he felt. "Did your mother leave him?" he asked.

She averted her face. She couldn't bear to talk about it yet. "In a way," she said huskily. "Are you going to drive me?" she added, glancing at him over her shoulder. "The bus doesn't run for another thirty minutes."

"Sure," he agreed.

"Then I'll get my jacket and purse."

She went into another room and came back quickly, leading the way out the door. "Is he conscious now?"

"Very," he murmured dryly. "When I left him, he was telling a nurse what she could do with the wash basin, and how far."

She chuckled. "He didn't seem like that kind of man," she murmured. "I had him figured for a gentleman, not a renegade."

"We're all that kind of man," he replied.

"All?"

He led her to the car and put her into the passenger seat. "There are five of us. The other three are coming up this morning to have a talk with the police."

"I remember. You said that your brother was the attorney general."

"He is," he replied. "We tend to stick together."

Her eyes went to his hands on the steering wheel. He had nice hands, very lean and strong with neat, clean fingernails. He was a tough-looking man, like a cowboy.

"How's your face?" he asked unexpectedly.

She shrugged. "It still hurts. It will for a while, but I'll be fine."

"You should see that plastic surgeon."

"Why?" she asked heavily. "My insurance won't pay for cosmetic surgery, and there's not much chance that they can do any major repair on tiny shattered bones."

"You're not a doctor. Stop giving yourself medical advice."

She stared at him for a long moment and started to speak, then lost the opportunity when he pulled up in the hospital parking lot, cut off the engine, and got out.

Rey waited for her and led her up to the floor where his brother's room was located.

Leo wasn't alone. Three other men were with him, one big and dark and missing an arm, the other lean and light-eyed and handsome, and a third big one with black eyes and a threatening face towering over both the others.

"That's Cag," Rey indicated the black-eyed man. "Corrigan," he nodded toward the light-eyed man, "and that's Simon," he finished, smiling at the one-armed man. "This is Meredith Johns. She rescued Leo."

"Nice to see you and know who you are," Leo said, alert now and interested as his dark eyes swept over the neat woman just inside the door. "Miss Johns, I presume?"

She smiled self-consciously, because everybody was looking at her bruised face. "Yes," she said.

Simon Hart frowned when he got a good look at her. "What the hell happened to you?" he demanded.

"Her father," Rey said for her. "She got in late and he beat her up."

Leo looked suddenly as intimidating as the other three. "Where is he?" he asked.

"In jail," Meredith said heavily. "For several weeks, at least, and he'll have time to dry out."

"Good." Leo looked toward Simon. "Maybe you can find a way to get him into rehab before he gets out."

"I'll look into it," Simon said at once.

"And some counseling wouldn't come amiss," Rey put his two cents worth in.

"I'll see about that, too," Simon replied. "Nice to meet you, Miss Johns. We're all grateful for what you did for Leo."

"You're all very welcome," she replied. She clutched her purse, intimidated by the group of brothers.

"Come here," Leo said, holding out his hand. "They're big and they look tough, but they're really marshmallows. You don't have to feel threatened. I'll protect you."

"She doesn't need protecting from us!" Rey snapped.

The others gaped at him. It wasn't like Rey to act that way.

He cleared his throat. He didn't want them asking themselves embarrassing questions about his attitude. He shoved his hands into his pockets. "Sorry. I didn't sleep much last night," he explained.

Meredith went to stand beside Leo, who took one of her small, cold hands in his and looked up at her with interest.

"Have you seen a doctor?" he asked.

"Your brother took me to the emergency room yesterday," she said.

"Rey. His name's Reynard, but he's called Rey," Leo informed her.

She smiled. "You look much better today. Head hurt?"

"A bit, but my vision's clear and I'm not disoriented," he said, quoting the doctor. "I have a good prognosis."

"That's nice to hear. You were in pretty bad shape."

"I'd have been in a lot worse shape, but for you," Leo said. "I hear that you can't work out in public for a while, until your face heals," he added. "Can you cook?"

She blinked. "Of course," she said at once.

"Can you make bread?"

She frowned. "Bread?"

"More specifically, biscuits," he added, and had the oddest expression on his face.

She shifted her purse in the hand he wasn't holding. "Well, yes, those and rolls and loaf bread," she said, as if everybody could do it.

Leo shot a glance at Rey, who was just staring at him without daring to say a word. He knew what was coming, and he couldn't decide how he felt about it. He didn't want to think about it.

"How would you like a brief stay in Jacobsville, Texas, in a big sprawling ranch house where your only job would be to make biscuits every morning?" Leo asked with his best smile.

Rey and the other brothers were staring at her, waiting. She wondered why. And Rey was frowning, as if he didn't like the idea at all. Probably he still secretly thought she was a hooker. He couldn't seem to credit her with any sense of decency.

She thought about his attitude for a few seconds, and decided that it wouldn't be a bad idea to take the job, and show him that you really couldn't judge a book by its cover. It wouldn't hurt that arrogant cowboy to be taken down a step or two, and she was just the girl who could do it.

She smiled. It hurt her face, but what was a little pain for a good cause? She turned back to Leo. "Mr. Hart, I think I'd like that job very much!"

Three

"**G**ood for you!" Leo exclaimed, animated and smiling. "You won't be sorry, Meredith. Honest."

She smiled back at him. He was nice, like a big brother. She liked him already. "I can do housekeeping, too," she told him. "I'll earn my keep."

"You'll go on salary, of course," he insisted. "It won't be a holiday."

"Nothing is a holiday with those two," Simon murmured dryly. "They aren't kidding about biscuits. They'll run you crazy baking them."

Rey and Leo gave their brother a disgusted look.

Meredith grinned. "I don't mind," she assured Simon. "I love to cook."

"It won't be that hard," Leo promised, with another speaking glance at Simon. "We just love biscuits. But we'll make you feel right at home. Anything you need, you can have—a new stove..." he added mischievously.

She thought about her father and her job, and her smile

faltered. "I have to wrap up a few loose ends first," she began.

"No problem," Leo assured her. "I can't get out of here for another day at least, or so that doctor said," he added with impatience.

"You'll stay until he lets you out," Rey said firmly. "Concussions are tricky. You know that."

Leo grimaced. "I guess so. I hate hospitals."

"I'm not too wild about them myself," Rey had to agree.

"It would be a very sad world without them," Meredith spoke up.

She seemed irritated, Rey thought, and wondered why. "I'll run you back home when you're ready," Rey told her. "We'll be in touch before we're ready to leave."

"All right." She held Leo's hand again and squeezed it gently, to the amusement of all the Harts except Rey. "You get better. I'll see you soon."

"Thanks again," Leo told her with genuine gratitude.

"It was nothing." She gave him another smile, tugged her hand free, and let Rey herd her out the door after a quick goodbye to the other brothers.

"I thought your brother was big until I saw all of you together. Goodness, you're all huge!" she exclaimed when they were outside in the parking lot. She gave him a long scrutiny. "And there doesn't seem to be an extra ounce of fat on any of you."

"We don't sit behind desks. We're ranchers, not office workers, and we work hard, right alongside our cowboys," he said. His dark eyes cut sideways. "Leo likes you."

She smiled. "I'm glad, because I like him, too."

That set him off and he tried not to let it show. He didn't want her to like Leo. He wished he knew why. He glanced at her as he wove skillfully through traffic toward her house. "Do you have family besides your father?" he asked.

"A cousin or two near Fort Worth," she said. She

glanced out the window, absently rubbing the ring finger of her left hand, trying not to choke up over the question. "What is Jacobsville like?" she asked to divert him from any further questions.

"It's small," he said easily. "There are a lot of ranches in the area. We have good pasture and soil, and we get enough rain to manage healthy crops." He grinned. "A lot of us are heavily into organic cattle raising. And with the industry under threat right now, we'll probably keep our financial heads above water when some other ranchers are going under."

"I like organic food," she said. "It may have a few more blemishes and bug bites, but if it doesn't kill bugs, it won't kill me," she added with a grin.

He chuckled. "Good point. Do you like animals?"

"I love them. I'd like to have a cat, but it's not possible. Dad's allergic to them." She sighed wearily, leaning her head back against the headrest. Her bruises were still giving her a lot of pain. Her hand went to them and she winced.

"You should see that plastic surgeon," he reminded her.

She shook her head. "Can't afford it. Even if I could, I don't want to go through weeks of surgery."

He hesitated and then he shrugged. "Have it your way."

"I'll heal." She touched her cheek again self-consciously. "I'm not sure going to work for you is a good idea. I mean, people might think the five of you beat me up!"

He laughed wholeheartedly. "Nobody who knows us would ever think that. Especially," he added, "if you can bake. Simon was right. I'm afraid we're famous locally for our addiction to biscuits."

Actually they were famous a lot further out than Jacobsville, but he didn't want to make her think they were loopy.

She took the words at face value. "I like to cook."

He glanced at her again, taking in her very conservative

way of dressing. "You don't look like the same woman I met just after Leo was assaulted."

"I almost never dress up," she confided. "And it really was a costume," she pointed out. "I wasn't lying. I don't make my living on the streets."

"How old are you?"

Her eyebrows arched. "Old enough."

"Are you over twenty-one?" he persisted.

"I'm twenty-three, almost twenty-four," she replied.

"And not married?"

"I've had responsibilities for the past few years," she said distantly, staring out the windshield. "My father has become the largest of them. I've been afraid to leave him alone."

"He's obviously dangerous when he drinks."

She hesitated, fingering her purse. "He seemed to lose himself in the bottle overnight. I thought I could handle him, control him, break the cycle. I couldn't even get help for him. My father doesn't think he has a drinking problem, so nobody would take him." She looked over at him. "I'm very grateful to your brother for his help. As I mentioned the night he was arrested, my father has only been like this for the past few months. It's not a long-standing problem. But I couldn't solve it alone."

"You're going to work for us," Rey said. "And it's not that much of a problem for Simon. He's good at his job."

"Is it a big ranch?" she asked unexpectedly.

"Enormous," he replied, "and one of five ranches we own as a family. Things get hectic during roundup, as you'll find out if you're still there next Spring."

"I won't be," she said with some certainty. "When I heal, I have to get back to my job."

"What do you do?" he asked curiously. "Is it house-cleaning or working as a cook in a restaurant?"

She almost bit her tongue at the demeaning comment. "You don't think I'm qualified to do anything else?"

He averted his eyes to the road. "I don't know you, Miss Johns," he commented carelessly. "But you seem pretty domestic to me."

She didn't feel well enough to retaliate. But one day, she promised herself, she was going to make him eat those condescending words.

"I've made beds and done light cleaning," she said, talking around her actual profession.

"Aren't you ambitious?" he persisted, with a faint frown. "Most women are, these days."

"That sounded bitter," she commented. "Did you get thrown over by an ambitious woman?"

"By a couple of them," he said curtly, and his expression became hard.

She hadn't thought of him that way. They'd been adversaries from the first contact. But it occurred to her as she gave him a quick, covert scrutiny, that he was a sensuous man. He wasn't handsome—except for Corrigan Hart, the rest of the brothers seemed cursed by a lack of conventional good looks.

But Rey had a lithe, graceful stride, and a strong face. He had good hands, clean and long-fingered. She liked the blackness of his straight hair, the high cheekbones, the long, thin, chiseled mouth. He was the sort of man who could have attracted women, except for his personality. The Harts didn't strike her as particularly gregarious or good mixers from her brief acquaintance with them. Leo was the one with the warmest personality. He made her feel at ease. The man beside her made her uncomfortable, insecure, nervous. She wasn't usually so strung-out by a man's proximity. Not that she'd had a lot to do with men in very recent years. Her father's overprotective, possessive nature had seen to that. He'd been so certain that she was going to end up like her mother.

She closed her eyes briefly, hating the memories.

"If you want to go and see your father before we leave for Jacobsville, I'll ask Simon to arrange it."

She stiffened. "I don't want to see him again until he's sober," she replied. "We both need time to get over what happened."

"Is your face the only place he hit you?" he asked unexpectedly.

"He got me in the back and the side, too, but those were only bruises. The doctor checked me over thoroughly." She sighed wearily. "I'm so tired," she murmured absently.

"I'm not surprised. You can get some rest. I'll phone you tomorrow, when we'll know more about Leo's condition and when he'll be released."

"Okay."

He stopped in front of her house and parked the car, walking to the door with her. He looked down at her while she fumbled the key into the lock. She was, in some ways, the most vulnerable woman he'd ever met. But there was steel in her makeup. He sensed that she wasn't like this usually, that she was fiery and independent and determined.

"This isn't the first time your father's laid into you, is it?" he asked suddenly.

She glanced at him, surprised. "No. But until this happened, it was more humiliating than painful." She frowned. "How did you know?"

He seemed concerned. "When I was in school, I had a couple of friends whose fathers got violent during binges. There's an...attitude, a posture, that people get when they've been beaten. I can't explain it, but I recognize it when I see it."

"Do you want to know what it is?" she asked with a world-weary smile. "It's a feeling of futility, of knowing that no matter what you do, you can't hold out physically against a man who's enraged and bent on hurting you. Because you know if you fight back, it will be even worse, maybe fatally worse. I don't like it," she added, her pale eyes beginning to glow, "and he's never getting the chance to do this again. He's my father. I love him, and I feel sorry for him. But I'm nobody's victim. Not even his."

He pushed his hands into his slacks' pockets and smiled at her. Her face was bright with color, and her eyes were alive, like peridots in sunlit water. He remembered her long blond hair around her shoulders and he wondered what she'd look like in pink silk. The thought shocked him and he scowled.

"Did I glue my nose on upside down?" she asked, raising her eyebrows.

He let out a short laugh. "No. I had a wild thought. Do you need an advance on your salary? I mean, is there anything you have to get for the trip that you can't afford?"

"I don't have a car," she began, and hated remembering why.

He glared. "I didn't say you were going to have to get to Jacobsville on your own. You'll go with Leo and me. Simon drove my car up from Jacobsville."

"Do I get to ride in the car, or have you got me earmarked for the trunk?" she returned.

He pursed his lips. Odd feelings were kindling inside him. "Keep that up and you'll be riding on the back bumper."

She wrinkled her nose. "Nice. Real nice. I can see you're going to be a great boss."

"If you don't burn the biscuits, I will be," he said.

"I'll stick close to your brother," she promised. "He'll protect me."

He didn't like that, but he wasn't going to let it show. "Leo's a tease," he said flatly. "Don't get your hopes up. He's not a marrying man. Neither am I," he added deliberately.

Her eyes widened. "Well, gee whiz, that's a major disappointment! And to think, I was only willing to take the job because of the marriage prospects!"

His face shuttered. "Sarcasm doesn't get you any points with me. I'm just making the position clear. We need a cook, not a prospective soul mate."

"Speak for yourself," she told him, turning back to her door. "I think Leo likes me already."

"I just told you...!"

She opened the door and looked back at him with pure irreverence. "Your brother can speak for himself. You don't own him, and you don't own me. I'll do what I please."

"Damn it...!"

"With charm like that, it's no surprise to me that you're still single," she said as she walked into the house.

"I can be charming when I've got a reason to be," he said icily. "But that's something you'll never know!"

"Lucky me!"

He started to speak, closed his lips tight, and walked back to his car.

She closed the door quickly and leaned back against it, almost shivering with anger. Of all the conceited, infuriating men she'd ever met, that one took the cake!

The next day, Rey phoned her midmorning to tell her that he and Leo would pick her up at one for the drive down to Jacobsville.

She had her suitcase packed and the house closed up when the big luxury car pulled into the driveway. It was a late-model car, and it looked odd, sitting in front of the shabby little house.

As she walked to the car, Meredith saw curtains fluttering and knew that the neighbors were getting an eyeful. They probably thought she was being carried off by the mob. That amused her and she smiled, glad that something diverted her mind from her father and her pain, and the misery of the past few months.

"We hadn't planned to ask you to help us move cattle,"

Rey drawled when he saw how she was dressed, in jeans and a striped shirt and boots.

"I haven't volunteered, either," she assured him. "But I didn't think you'd want me to do housework in a dress." She gave him a wry glance. "Those old black-and-white sitcoms weren't historically accurate, you know. I never saw a woman vacuum the carpet wearing a dress and high heels and pearls!"

"You can do housework in a suit for all I care, as long as you can bake me a pan of biscuits every morning," Rey said, taking the suitcase and putting it in the trunk.

"Good morning," Leo called from the open window of the front seat, grinning as Rey opened the back door and helped her inside.

"Good morning," she said brightly. "You look much better."

"I feel better, except for the headache." He gave her a long look. "You aren't in very good shape yourself. Face hurt?"

"Yes. I guess we're both like walking wounded, huh?" she asked with a grin as she leaned back into the warm leather seat.

"Maybe we should take a nurse with us," Rey muttered as he got in and started the car.

Meredith cleared her throat, but before she could speak, Leo turned to his brother. "I don't need nursing, thank you very much!" Leo said curtly.

"Neither do I!" Meredith agreed.

Rey glanced at them as he pulled out into the street. "I've seen accident victims who looked better than the two of you."

"Don't let him insult you, Meredith," Leo told her. "I'll tell you all about his weak spots so that you can deal with him."

She wouldn't have expected Rey to have any of those, but she was keeping her mouth shut and her options open for the time being. Her new boss looked formidable, and even Leo seemed curious about his lack of warmth.

"Are you all from Jacobsville originally?" Meredith changed the subject.

"No, we're from San Antonio," Leo said. "We inherited the Jacobsville property and it needed a lot of work, so we made it our headquarters. It's convenient to Houston and San Antonio, and frankly, it's isolated and gives us some privacy. We don't like cities as a rule."

"Neither do I," she said, recalling her grandmother's beautiful flower garden at the old place near Fort Worth. She smiled. "I wish Dad hadn't taken the job in Houston in the first place."

"What does he do?" Leo asked.

"He's retired," she said, not wanting to go into specifics. It hurt to talk about her family. Her father was a sore spot just now, anyway.

"Simon talked to the authorities," Rey interrupted. "They're going to make sure he gets counseling and he won't be released until he's kicked the alcohol habit." He glanced over the seat at her, his dark eyes intent. "They think it will be better if you don't have any contact with him for a few weeks, until he's through the worst of the withdrawal symptoms."

"I know about withdrawal," she replied, absently smoothing her hand over her jeans. "Bad habits are hard to break, even new ones."

"You two must read a lot," Rey replied. "I never saw so many books in one place as I did at your house. Even our library isn't that stuffed, and we all read."

"I love reading," she agreed. "We have a television, but neither of us had much time to watch it. Until recently," she added reluctantly, and winced at the thoughts that went through her mind. "I hope they get those men who mugged you, Mr. Hart," she told Leo fervently.

"Leo," he corrected. "It's really Leopold, but nobody

calls me that," he added with a grin. "We're pretty informal with our employees."

"Do you have a lot?" she asked curiously.

"A good many in Jacobsville," he replied. "Although we don't have a full-time vet, we do have several accountants, livestock managers, computer programmers, salesmen…you name it, we've got one. It's big business these days to run cattle. We even have a man who does nothing but keep up with legislation that may impact us."

"Do you have dogs and cats?" she asked.

"Always," Rey replied. "We have border collies that help us herd cattle, and we keep cats in the barn to help handle the rats."

"We had a cat in the house," Leo added, "but it was Cag and Tess's, and they took it with them when they moved into their new house. At least she won't have to cope with Herman," he told his brother, and laughed.

Rey smiled involuntarily. "You might not have wanted to work for us if we still had Herman."

"Who's Herman?" she wanted to know.

"He was Cag's albino python," he told her. "He weighed a hundred and ten pounds and lived in a cage in Cag's bedroom. He gave Herman up when he married Tess. He said it would be crazy to keep an animal that big and dangerous around their son. They're still over the moon about that little boy."

"Yes, but there are people who don't even consider things like that," Meredith murmured absently. "I remember a little girl who had to have plastic surgery because she was bitten in the face by her father's pet boa constrictor."

"Herman didn't bite, but Tess almost had a heart attack when she first came to work for us and found him in the washing machine."

"I can sympathize with her," Meredith said. "I haven't come across many snakes. I'm not sure I want to."

"We have rattlers and water moccasins around the

place," Rey told her. "You have to watch where you walk, but we've only had one person bitten in recent years. Snakes are always going to be a hazard in open country. You can't be careless."

"I'll remember."

"We've got a big garage apartment," Leo told her. "It's got picture windows and a whirlpool bath. Tess lived there until she and Cag married. I think you'll like it."

"I don't mind where I stay," she said easily. "I'm grateful to have a job at all. I really couldn't go to work in Houston looking like this. It would have been embarrassing for my boss."

"You won't have people staring at you on the ranch," Leo assured her. "And it won't take too long for those bruises to heal."

"I'll be fine, but you'll have to take it easy for a few days still, I'm sure they told you that," she returned at once. "No violent exertion. Concussion is tricky."

"I know that," Leo told her. "We had a man who was kicked in the head by a horse. He dropped dead three days later while he was walking into the corral. It was a hard lesson about head injuries. None of us ever forgot it."

She averted her eyes. She didn't like thinking about head injuries just now.

"I've got to stop for gas," Rey said as they reached the outskirts of the city and he pulled into a self-service gas station. "Anybody want something to drink?"

"Coffee for me," Leo said. "Meredith?"

"I'd like a small coffee, black, please."

"I'll go get it after I fill the tank," Rey said. He got out and started pumping gas.

Leo leaned his arm over the back seat and looked at Meredith openly, his dark eyes quiet and gently affectionate.

"You're still having a hard time with Rey, aren't you?" he asked her.

"He doesn't really like me," she confessed with a wry smile. "And I have to admit, he puts my back up, too. He seems to want to think the worst of me. He was convinced that I mugged you."

He chuckled. "You aren't tall enough to have knocked me out," he said. "But Rey doesn't like women much. He had a bad time of it with a young woman who turned out to be a call girl," he added, noticing absently how stunned Meredith seemed to be at that remark. "He had the ring bought, the honeymoon spot picked out, and then he found out the truth about her. It took him years to get over it. He was crushed."

"I guess so," she said heavily. "Good Lord, no wonder he thought the worst when he saw how I was dressed."

Leo frowned. "I just barely remember the rig you had on. What was it, some sort of costume?"

"I'd been to a wild Halloween party and had just escaped when I saw those men bending over you," she told him. "I ran at them waving my arms and yelling, and frightened them off."

"That was taking a hell of a chance!" he exploded.

She shrugged. "I've done it before," she said. "I learned it from my...from my brother's best friend," she amended, forcing the words out. It was much too soon to try to talk about her tragedy. "He taught karate in the military. He said that sometimes all it needed was a yell and the element of surprise to spook an attacker and make him run. It works."

"Not all the time," Leo said darkly, "and not for women. I'm all for equality, but most men are bigger and stronger than most women, and in hand-to-hand, you'd lose. You can't count on a man running, loud noise or not."

"Well, it worked for you," she amended, and smiled at him. "I'm glad, because I couldn't have wrestled those guys down."

He nodded. "See that you remember it," he told her. "Don't take chances. Get help."

"Some help those partygoers would have been," she scoffed. "Half of them were drunk, and the other half probably wouldn't have walked across the street to save a grandmother from a mugging!"

"Then why were you at a party with them?" he asked reasonably.

She picked at a fingernail. "A girl I know from work said I needed a night off and insisted that I come. I wore an old costume, the only one I had, and thought I'd enjoy myself. I don't do drugs or drink, and one of the men made a blatant pass at me." She wrapped her arms around her body in a defensive posture that betrayed her fear. "I was anxious to get away from the whole mess, luckily for you," she added with a grin.

"I don't like parties much, either," he said. "Getting drunk isn't my idea of a good time."

She glanced out the window. Rey had finished pumping gas and was inside the convenience store now. "Does he drink?" she asked.

"Very rarely. I've been known to, under provocation, but Rey's levelheaded and sober. He can be mean, and he's got the blackest temper of all of us, but he's a good man to have on your side when the chips are down."

"He doesn't like me," she repeated.

"He'll come around, give him time," Leo told her. "Meanwhile, you've got a job and a place to stay while your face heals. We all have hard times," he added gently. "But we get through them, even when we don't expect to. Give yourself time."

She smiled. "Thanks," she said huskily. "You really are a nice man."

"Nice, clean, sober, modest and incredibly handsome," he added with a wicked grin. "And I haven't even gotten to my best points yet!"

"Compared to your brothers," she began, "you—"

The door opened before she could hang herself, and Rey shoved a cup of coffee at her before he handed the second one to Leo.

"It's hot," he told them as he slid in and took the soft drink out of his jacket pocket and put it in the cup holder.

"Cold caffeine," Leo said, shuddering. "Why can't you drink coffee like a normal man?"

"I drink coffee at breakfast," Rey told him haughtily.

"So do I, but you don't have to have rules on when to drink it!"

Rey started the engine with a speaking glance.

"See that look?" Leo indicated it to Meredith. "When he looks like that, you've already lost whatever argument you're in the middle of. We call it 'the look.' I once saw him break up a fistfight with it."

"I don't plan to argue," Meredith promised.

Rey gave her "the look," and it lingered before his attention turned back to the windshield.

Meredith sat back against the leather seat and wondered suddenly if she wasn't making the biggest mistake of her life.

Four

The Hart Ranch was almost as Meredith had pictured it, with neat wooden fences concealing electrified fencing, improved pasture land and cattle everywhere. There were also pastures with horses, and there was a barn big enough to store a commercial jet. But she loved the house itself, with its graceful arches reminiscent of Spanish architecture, and the incredible number of small trees and shrubs around it. In the spring, it must be glorious. There were two ponds, a decorative one in the front of the house and a larger one behind the house in which a handful of ducks shivered in the November sun.

"Do you have goldfish in the pond?" she asked excitedly as Rey stopped the car in front of the house on an inlaid stone driveway.

"Goldfish and Koi," he answered, smiling reluctantly at her excitement. "We have a heater in the pond to keep them comfortable during the winter. There are water lilies in there, too, and a lotus plant."

"Does the other pond have goldfish, too, where the ducks are?" she wondered.

Leo chuckled. "The other one is because of the ducks. We had to net this pond to keep them out of it so we'd *have* some goldfish. The ducks were eating them."

"Oh, I see." She sighed. "It must be beautiful here in the spring," she said dreamily, noting the gazebo and the rose garden and stone seats and shrubs around the goldfish pond.

"It's beautiful to us year-round," Leo told her with lazy affection. "We all love flowers. We've got some more roses in a big flower garden around the back of the house, near a stand of pecan trees. Tess is taking courses in horticulture and she works with hybrids."

"I love roses," Meredith said softly. "If I had time, I'd live in a flower garden."

"I suppose cleaning rooms is time-consuming," Rey murmured sarcastically as he got out of the car and went in the front door of the house.

Leo glanced at her curiously while Rey was out of earshot. "You clean rooms?"

"I don't," she told him with a sharp grin. "But I'm living down to your brother's image of my assets."

Leo pursed his lips. "Now, that's interesting. You sound like a woman with secrets."

"More than you'd guess," she told him heavily. "But none that I'm ashamed of," she added quickly, just in case he got the wrong idea.

"Rey doesn't like you, does he?" he murmured, almost to himself. "I wonder why? It's not like him to pick on sick people."

"I'm not sick," she assured him. "I'm just battered, but I'll heal."

"Sure you will," Leo promised, smiling. "You'll be safe here. The only real chore you'll have is baking. By the time you're completely back on your feet, your father will be sober and in counseling, and your home life will have changed drastically.''

''I hope so,'' she said huskily.

He watched her eyes grow tragic and haunted. He frowned. ''Meredith,'' he said slowly. ''If you need to talk, ever, I can listen without making judgments.''

She met his clear dark eyes. ''Thanks, Leo,'' she said with genuine gratitude. ''But talking won't change a thing. It's a matter of learning to live with…things.''

''Now I'm intrigued.''

''Don't push,'' she said gently. ''I'm not able to talk about my problems yet. They're too fresh. Too painful.''

''And more than just your father, or I'm a dirt farmer,'' he drawled.

She shrugged. ''Perhaps.''

''Anyway, just take your time and let the world pass you by. You're going to love it here. I promise.''

''Am I?'' She watched Rey come back out of the house with an elderly lady in tow, wringing her hands on her apron.

''That's Mrs. Lewis,'' Leo told her. ''We talked her into coming back to bake biscuits for us, even though she'd retired, but now we're losing her to arthritis. She's going to show you the ropes. But not right now,'' he added quickly.

''No time like the present,'' Meredith disagreed with a smile. ''Busy hands make busy minds.''

''I know how that works,'' Leo murmured drolly.

Rey opened the back door and helped Meredith out. ''Mrs. Lewis, this is Meredith Johns, our new cook. Meredith, Annie Lewis. She's retiring. Again.'' He made it sound like a shooting offense.

''Oh, my, yes, I'm losing the use of my hands, I'm afraid,'' Mrs. Lewis said. ''Glad to meet you, Miss Johns.''

''Glad to meet you, too, Mrs. Lewis,'' Meredith replied.

"I'll take your bag to your room, while Mrs. Lewis shows you around the house," Rey added.

"She just got here," Leo protested.

"And there's no time like the present to show her the house," Rey replied.

"That's just what she said," Leo sighed.

Rey glanced at Meredith, who gave him a wicked grin and followed along behind Annie Lewis, who was making a valiant effort not to ask about the terrible bruises on Meredith's face.

"It's a big, sprawling house, and it takes a lot of cleaning," Mrs. Lewis said as she led Meredith down the long hall and opened doors to the very masculine bedrooms both with dark, heavy Mediterranean furniture and earth tones in the drapes and carpets. "The men aren't messy, thank God, but they track in all that mud and dust and animal fur! They had beige carpeting when I came here." She glanced at Meredith with a shake of her head. "Red mud just won't come *out* of beige carpet!"

"Or anything else," Meredith added on a soft laugh.

"They work hard, and they're away a lot. But the foreman lives in the bunkhouse with a couple of bachelor cowboys, and they'll look out for you."

"I don't know that I'll be here very long," Meredith replied quietly. "They offered me the job so that I can have time for these to heal." She touched her face, and looked straight at the older woman, who was struggling not to ask the question in her eyes.

"Nobody will hurt you here," Mrs. Lewis said firmly.

Meredith smiled gently. "My father got drunk and beat me up, Mrs. Lewis," she explained matter-of-factly. "He's a good and kind man, but we've had a terrible tragedy to work through. He hasn't been able to cope with it except by losing himself in a bottle, and now he's gone too far and he's in jail." She sighed. "I tried so hard to help him. But I couldn't."

Mrs. Lewis didn't say a word. She put her arms around Meredith and rocked her in them. The shock of it brought the tears that she'd held back for so long. She wept until her body shook with sobs.

Rey, looking for her, stopped dead in the doorway of his bedroom and met Mrs. Lewis's misty eyes over Meredith's bowed shoulders. It shocked him to see that feisty, strong woman collapsed in tears. It hurt him.

Mrs. Lewis made a gesture with her eyebrows and a severe look. Rey acknowledged it with a nod and a last glance at the younger woman as he walked back down the hall.

Supper was riotous. Meredith had made a huge pan of homemade biscuits and ferreted out all sorts of preserves to go with them. For an entrée, she made fajitas with lean beef and sliced vegetables, served with wild rice and a salad. Dessert was fresh fruit and fresh whipped cream, the only concession besides the biscuits that she made to fat calories. She'd also found some light margarine to set out.

"This is good," Rey commented as he glanced at her. "We usually have broiled or fried steak with lots of potatoes."

"Not bad once a week or so, but terrible for your cholesterol," she pointed out with a smile as she finished her salad. "Lean beef is okay for you, but not in massive doses."

"You sound like a dietician," Leo chuckled.

"Modern women have to keep up with health issues," she said evasively. "I'm responsible for your health while I'm working for you. I have to be food-conscious."

"That's fine," Rey told her flatly, "but don't put tofu and bean sprouts in front of me if you want to stay here."

Her eyebrows arched. "I hate tofu."

"Thank God," Leo sighed as he buttered another biscuit. "I got fed tofu salad the last time I went to Brewster's for supper," he added with absolute disgust. "I ate the olives and the cheese and left the rest."

"I can't say that I blame you," Meredith said, laughing because he looked so forlorn.

"Janie Brewster thinks tofu is good for him," Rey commented. "But she thinks he needs therapy more. He doesn't like fish. She says that has some sort of connection to his fear of deep water." He glanced at his brother with wicked affection. "She's a psychology major. She already has an associate degree from our local junior college."

"She's twenty," Leo said with a twist of his lower lip. "She knows everything."

"She just got her associate degree this spring," Rey added.

"Good. Maybe she'll get a job in New York," Leo said darkly.

"Why New York?" Meredith asked curiously.

"Well, it's about as far east as she can go and find her sort of work," Leo muttered. "And she'd be out of my hair!"

Rey gave him a covert glance and finished his fajitas.

Meredith finished her own meal and got up to refill coffee cups. She had a feeling that Leo was more interested in the nebulous Brewster girl than he wanted to admit.

"We need groceries," she told them when she'd served dessert and they were eating it. "Mrs. Lewis made me a list."

"You can use one of the ranch trucks to drive to town," Leo suggested carelessly.

Her fingers toyed with her fork. "I haven't driven in several months."

"You don't drive?" Rey exclaimed, shocked.

She couldn't meet his eyes. "I take buses." Cars made her feel guilty.

"Why?"

She remembered a day she should have driven. The memories were horrible…

"Meredith, it's all right," Leo said gently, sensing something traumatic about her behavior. "I'll drive you. Okay?"

"You won't," Rey replied. "You're in worse shape than she is. Which brings up another point. You don't need to be walking around town like that," he told her.

She wasn't offended; it was a relief. She even smiled. "No, I don't guess I do. Will you do the shopping?" she asked him, her wide, soft eyes steady on his.

He felt wild little thrills shooting through his body at the impact. It had been years since he'd been so shaken by eye contact alone. He didn't move. He just stared at her, his dark eyes unblinking, curious. His body rippled with vague hunger.

Leo, watching the eye contact, tried not to grin. He cleared his throat, and Rey seemed to remember that he had a forkful of fruit halfway to his mouth. He took it the rest of the way and chewed it carefully before he spoke.

"I'll get the groceries," Rey volunteered. He glared at both of them, noting the shaved place where Leo had stitches near the back of his head. "Obviously I'm the only one here who can walk around without drawing curious stares from bystanders!"

Leo buttered another biscuit. "That sounds like sour grapes to me. If you want attention, try walking around without your pants."

"I didn't say I wanted attention," Rey returned hotly.

"Good thing." He glanced at Meredith with a mischievous smile. "He looks like hell without his pants," he said conversationally. "Hairiest legs of the bunch."

"That's debatable," Rey shot back. "Yours aren't much better."

"What a good thing you two aren't Scottish," Meredith said demurely.

It took a minute for them to get it, then Leo burst out

laughing, trying to picture his younger brother in a kilt. Rey lifted a corner of his thin mouth, but he wasn't in a smiling mood. It bothered him, that Meredith had been crying in Mrs. Lewis's arms, that she didn't drive, that she was so mysterious about her life. She was twenty-three, almost twenty-four. Most women by that age had been involved in a serious relationship, some more than one. Many had been married.

His heart skipped. Was that her secret? He remembered watching her rub her ring finger in the car. He glanced at it curiously. She didn't wear a ring, and there was no sign that she'd been wearing one there. She didn't act married. She hadn't talked about having a husband. She was single, apparently by choice. But had there been men in her past? He was still carrying scars from his one great love affair, from the deception he'd endured. Meredith had gone out walking to a party in a rig that made her look like a prostitute, and she'd been comfortable doing that. It wasn't something an innocent girl would have considered.

Knowing that, he looked at her in a different way, speculatively. She had a nice figure and she wasn't all flushing smiles like Janie Brewster when Leo was around. Meredith was oddly mature for her age, almost matronly. She seemed to be used to giving instructions, too. She was a puzzle that disturbed him. What if she was hiding something sordid in her past? He and Leo had taken her in on faith and pity, but now he wondered if they'd made a terrible mistake. If she were in league with the men who'd robbed Leo, they might have a dangerous situation developing. What if she'd planned the whole thing as a means to an end?

Basically Rey didn't trust her. He wasn't going to let down his guard, either, no matter if looking at her did raise his blood pressure. She wasn't going to know that she did. And he'd keep his eyes open, all the time, just in case.

The days turned to a week. Meredith's painful bruises faded slowly. She lost some of the brooding sadness that seemed to cling to her like the jeans she wore around the house when she was working. She found the slower, easier pace strange, and she missed the urgency of her daily routine. But as the days went by lazily, she realized that she hadn't really given herself time to think. She'd avoided it, ignored it, hoping that the past would vanish. Now she was face to face with it, forced to reflect on what had happened.

She sat beside the fishpond one sunny afternoon, between chores, and watched the goldfish under the surface of the dark water as they moved sluggishly. The water wasn't frozen, but it was cold. The pond heater only kept a small area heated, so the fish were limited in movement. She could imagine how it would be to sit here in the summer and watch them move around in their watery world, with flowers blooming all around.

She'd loved planting flowers. She missed her home, her bulbs and shrubs, the familiar things that she'd accumulated around her. Now it was all gone, sold without a second thought to make the memories bearable. It was too late, and she wished she'd been more sensible. There were things she should have kept. Mike's stupid baseball cap, the one he always wore on the rare occasions when he wasn't working, and when he went fishing. She missed her mother's collection of small silk Chinese boxes and her pretty evening gowns. She'd thrown all those things away. At the time, it had seemed reasonable to cut all the ties with the past. It didn't, now.

The sound of a truck pulling up to the front door caught her attention. Rey and Leo had been out of town for two days, attending another cattle convention, this time in Denver.

They climbed out of the cab of the big six-wheeled pickup truck and retrieved their suitcases from the back, waving as the ranch truck pulled right out again and took off down the road.

Meredith got up and went to join them.

"Want some coffee and pie?" she asked with a smile.

"That would really hit the spot," Leo said, returning the smile. "I hate commercial flights."

"You're the smart guy who said our jet needed to be overhauled," Rey reminded him.

"It did," Leo replied.

Rey was looking at Meredith openly. "The bruises are fading," he remarked. "You have more color, too."

"I've been getting out in the sunlight," she replied easily. "I like to watch the fish, even though they don't move much."

"We might put a big aquarium inside," Rey remarked, unaware of his brother's quick, curious glance. "I like fish myself."

"They've done studies," Meredith volunteered as they stood aside to let her enter the house first. "They say watching fish swim is calming. It helps relieve stress."

"God knows, we could use some of that," Leo chuckled. "Especially when cattle prices fall and feed prices go through the roof."

"Cattle raising must be a complex process," she remarked.

"Very complex," Rey said. He frowned as he watched her walk. "Hip sore?" he asked.

She laughed self-consciously. "Well, yes, it is. How did you know?"

"You've got a light limp on the right side. Barely noticeable."

She rubbed her hip self-consciously. "I fell on that side, the night Dad hit me," she told him. "The floor's pretty hard."

"There's a whirlpool bath in your bedroom," Rey reminded her. "It'll help the soreness."

"I discovered that," she said, grinning. "What a luxury! We only have a shower at home, and it's temperamental."

Rey gave her a long look. "When we've had time to

catch our breath, I'll see what I can find out about your father, if you'd like.''

Her face brightened. "That would be nice.''

He smiled slowly, liking the way her pale eyes seemed to glow when she was pleased. She wasn't bad-looking at all, and her figure was just about perfect. He wondered how she could have remained single for so long, with her home-making skills, not to mention her sweet personality and that knockout body.

She was watching him with equal appreciation, and totally unaware of it. He had a lithe, powerful physique that made her think of rodeo. He walked with a unique sort of grace, and he didn't stoop or slouch, ever. She liked his eyes best of all. They were almost a liquid-brown, and they had black rims around the pupils. He was rugged and sensuous, and she looked at his wide thin mouth and wondered for the first time how it would feel to kiss it.

Her thoughts horrified her. She dragged her eyes away and excused herself in an absolute fluster to go make coffee.

Leo lifted both eyebrows and stared at his brother after she was out of earshot. "Well, well,'' he murmured. "You do seem to be making an impression on her.''

"Cut it out,'' Rey said testily.

"And vice versa,'' came the irritating reply.

Rey made a rough sound in his throat and stomped off down the hall to his room. He put down his suitcase, took off his suit and dress shirt and got into jeans and a checked long-sleeved work shirt. He glanced at himself in the mirror as he buttoned it, his eyes blank as he recalled the wild flush on Meredith's cheeks. It shouldn't please him. He didn't trust her. She could be trying to play them all for suckers. But he smiled, just the same.

Meredith had coffee and cherry pie in saucers on the table by the time the brothers were changed and walking into the kitchen.

"Coffee's fresh," she said.

"Aren't you having any?" Rey asked.

"I have to get the clothes into the dryer," she excused herself with a quick smile. "Yell if you need anything."

She was gone in a flash.

Rey stared broodingly at his pie and frowned. She didn't want to have coffee with them. Why?

"You make her nervous," Leo said, answering the unspoken question. "She knows you don't trust her."

Rey frowned as he nibbled at his pie and sipped coffee. "I don't know her," he replied. He gave his brother a speaking glance. "We've always done background checks on employees," he added firmly. "I don't think we should make an exception of her, even though she's temporary."

"Translated, that means you want to know more about her than you do," Leo drawled, grinning.

"Maybe I do," Rey confessed. "But she's in a position to do a lot of damage if she isn't what she seems. You could have been killed, or suffered brain damage," he added quietly. "If she's in cahoots with the guys who mugged you..." He let the sentence trail off meaningfully.

Leo grimaced. "I don't like poking into peoples' private business," he replied. "But you're right. It's risky not to check her out."

"I'll get the agency on it first thing tomorrow," Rey said. He took another bite of the pie. "She's a hell of a good cook," he murmured.

"Makes good coffee, too," Leo commented.

They looked at each other and grimaced. It was going to upset Meredith if she found out what they were up to. But it was too much of a gamble not to find out what they could about her background and character. On the other hand, Leo promised himself, he was going to intercept that background check before Rey had a chance to see it. If Meredith had secrets she was hiding for a good reason, he wasn't going to give her away to Rey.

It took several days for the private detective to get to the case and send a report to the Harts.

Rey was out of town at a one-day seminar on a new spreadsheet computer program the brothers were using for herd records when the report arrived. Leo carried the report into his office and closed the door while he read it.

When he finished, he let out a harsh breath. So that was Meredith's secret. No wonder her father drank. No wonder she was so reticent and quiet about her past. He smiled as he considered her true profession, and he was determined that Rey wasn't going to know about it until disclosure was inevitable. Rey was too prone to conclusion-jumping and rushing to judgment. It was about time he had a set down, and Meredith was just the woman to give it to him. Meanwhile, he'd let Rey work on hanging himself. Obviously Meredith was enjoying her anonymity, and considering the high-powered pressures of her daily job, it wasn't surprising that she found mundane housekeeping a nice change. It wouldn't hurt to let her enjoy the vacation from stress, without probing into her feelings. No doubt she still felt the grief, even after several months.

He touched the report with idle fingers, frowning as he recognized one of the names on it. Mike had been a Houston policeman. He was also a friend of Colter Banks, a Texas Ranger and cousin of the Harts, who worked out of the Houston ranger office. It really was a small world. He wanted to tell Meredith that he remembered Mike, but he didn't want to blow her cover. He also didn't want her to know that they'd been checking up on her.

He put the file into the filing cabinet, deliberately putting it under the wrong letter of the alphabet. If Rey asked, he'd just tell him that the agency was working on it but had other, more urgent cases to assign agents to first.

*   *   *

Meredith was alone in the house when Rey came in, late that night, from his business trip. Leo had gone to dinner at the Brewsters' house again, presumably at the invitation of Janie's father, to talk about a new breeding bull the Brewsters were trying to sell him.

She'd just started the dishwasher and was ready to turn the lights off in the kitchen when she heard Rey come in.

He paused in the kitchen doorway, a black Stetson slanted over one dark eye, wearing a grey vested suit that clung lovingly to the hard, muscular lines of his tall body. Meredith felt ragged by comparison in her jeans and red T-shirt, and barefoot. Her hair was disheveled because she'd been scrubbing the floor with a brush, and she wasn't wearing makeup. She hadn't expected to see either of the brothers before she went to bed.

Rey's dark eyes went to her pretty feet and he smiled. "You don't like shoes, do you?"

She grimaced. "No, and it's not good to go without them. No arch support." She studied his lean face. He had dark circles under his eyes. "Would you like some coffee and something to eat?"

"I would," he said heavily. "They gave me peanuts on the plane," he added with absolute disgust.

She chuckled. The sound was pleasant, and Rey was surprised at how it touched him to hear her laugh.

"I'll make you a nice thick low-fat ham sandwich with sauce."

"Thanks," he said, sliding a chair out so that he could straddle it. He tossed his hat into the chair beside him and ran a hand through his thick dark hair. "Make the coffee first, Meredith. I've got paperwork that has to be done tonight before the accountant comes to do the books in the morning."

"Can't it wait?" she asked gently. "You look worn to a frazzle. You need an early night."

His eyes searched hers intently. "I don't need mothering," he said, angered out of all proportion.

She flushed and turned away. She didn't apologize or say another word, but her hands shook as she filled the coffeepot and started it brewing.

Rey cursed himself silently for snapping at her. It was unkind, especially after she'd volunteered to feed him. She'd been working hard, too, he could see the spotless floor and the brush and bucket she'd been using on it. She must have done it on her hands and knees. It was a big kitchen, too. He wasn't the only one who was tired.

He got up from the chair and moved to stand just behind her. His lean hands caught her small waist and pulled her back against him. "I'm sorry," he said, his voice deep and husky with sudden emotion.

Her cold fingers came to rest on his and her whole body went rigid as a flash of white-hot pleasure shot through it. She caught her breath. He heard it. His own body tautened and the hands around her waist suddenly grew possessive, rough, insistent, as they pulled her tight against him.

He could hear her breathing change. He could feel the faint tremor of her hands over his. Impulsively he bent his head and his mouth touched the side of her neck.

Five

Meredith knew her knees were shaking. She hoped she wasn't going to fall on the floor at his feet with sheer excitement. It had been years since a man had made her feel such a rush of pleasure, and even then, it had been one-sided. She'd been crazy about a man who only saw her as a sort of unrelated sister. But even that wasn't as powerful as what she was feeling with Rey Hart.

His mouth became insistent as it moved slowly up her neck. He began to turn her, in the silence that was suddenly alive with passion. His hard lips traveled to the hollow of her throat, where a tiny pulse hammered, and then up to her chin. His teeth nibbled her chin, moving on to her lower lip. He tugged it away from the top one and tasted it with his tongue. All the while, his lean, strong hands were sliding up and down at her waist, smoothing her body completely against him.

His teeth nipped at her top lip with a sensual approach that made her breath shiver in her throat. He was experienced, far more so than she was. For all her professional capability, in this way she was a novice, and it showed.

He noticed her lack of sensual response with absent curiosity. She was attracted to him, that was obvious, but it was as if she didn't know what to do.

He guided her hands to his vest and flicked open buttons while his lips teased around hers. She fumbled and he laughed softly, his nose rubbing against hers as he moved her hands and unfastened the buttons on his vest and shirt with deft efficiency. He coaxed her hands inside, against thick hair and hard, warm muscle, while his mouth began to bite at hers, tempting her lips to part. She was stiff, trying not to respond, but her body was hungry.

"Like this," he whispered gently, teaching her mouth the lazy, sensual rhythm he wanted from it. "Taste my mouth, the way I'm tasting yours. Don't fight what you're feeling."

She heard the words as if through a fog. She didn't understand what he was saying, but her body obeyed him. She was in a sensual limbo, her hands flat against his chest, her head lifted, her eyes slitted and looking up into his as he began to increase the teasing pressure of his mouth. She followed his lips. She relaxed into the curve of his powerful body with a little shiver.

He devoured her mouth roughly, again and then again, tempting her until her mouth followed his, returning the arousing pressure. She could see the glitter grow in his narrow eyes, feel the grip of his lean hands as he pushed her hips against the sudden hardness of him. She gasped with embarrassment and then lost all sense of it as his mouth opened and pushed down hard against her parted lips, drowning her in passion.

It was like flying, she thought dazedly. He hesitated for an instant and her eyes opened, drowsy and curious. Her mouth was swollen, soft, tremulous. She looked at him with fascination, utterly helpless in his embrace. He felt an un-

familiar protectiveness toward her. It had been years since
he'd kissed an innocent. Meredith's lack of experience was
obvious. He was enjoying it.

"Yes," he murmured gruffly, and he bent again. His
arms enfolded her, tender arms that no longer forced her
into intimacy. His mouth was tender, too, exploring hers
with slow mastery, careful not to overwhelm her.

She sighed into his hard mouth, relaxing against him.
Her hands moved restlessly on his broad, bare chest, and
contracted in the thick mat of hair that covered him.

He lifted his head, staring down into her wide eyes with
somber delight. His hands smoothed hers deeper into his
thick hair and hard muscle. He traced the edges of her short
nails with his thumbs. His breath was jerky. He didn't like
having her see that he was vulnerable. There were too many
things he still didn't know about her, and he didn't trust
her. She seemed innocent, but he couldn't forget the dress
she'd been wearing and the accusations her father had made
about her. He didn't dare trust her on such short acquaintance. On the other hand, his body was singing with pleasure from the long, hot contact with hers. He couldn't force
himself to let her go. Not just yet.

"Why did you do that?" she asked huskily.

One dark eyebrow lifted. He didn't smile. "Why did you
let me?" he shot back.

She felt uncomfortable. Despite the effort it took, she
moved away from him. He let her go with no show of
reluctance. He watched her struggle for composure while
he refastened buttons with easy confidence, concealing the
effect she had on him. He didn't even look ruffled.

"The coffee must be done by now," he pointed out when
she seemed unable to move.

She turned stiffly and went to fill cups and put them,
along with cream and sugar, on the table.

While he fixed his coffee, she made him two thick ham
sandwiches with hands that slowly lost their tremor. She

was devastated by a kiss that didn't seem to have disturbed him at all. She remembered the sudden hardness of his body, but she knew all about anatomy. A man couldn't help that reaction to anything feminine, it was part of his makeup. It wasn't even personal.

Somehow, it made things worse to know that. She felt his eyes on her back, and she knew he was measuring her up. She had no idea why he'd kissed her, but she didn't trust his motives. He didn't like her. She couldn't afford to let her guard down. Rey Hart would be hell on a woman who loved him. She knew that instinctively.

By the time she had the sandwiches made, her hands were steady again and she was able to put them on the table with a cool smile.

"I have to tidy up the living room…" she began.

He caught her hand as she started past him. "Sit down, Meredith," he said quietly.

She sat. He sipped coffee and studied her for a long moment. "I talked to Simon while I was away," he said. "Your father has been released from jail and placed in an alcohol treatment center. It's early days yet, but the prognosis is good. It helps that he hasn't been drinking that heavily for a long time."

She looked relieved and anxiously waited to hear what else Rey had to say about her father.

He continued. "The therapist wouldn't reveal any intimate details to Simon, you understand, but he was able to say that your father had been unable to deal with a family tragedy. Now that he's sober, he's extremely upset about what he did to you." He looked grim. "He doesn't remember doing it, Meredith."

She averted her eyes to her coffee cup. For something to do, she lifted it and took a sip of blistering black coffee, almost burning her lip. "That's common in cases of alcohol or drug abuse," she murmured absently.

He studied her over the rim of his coffee cup. "You

won't be allowed to communicate with him until he's through the treatment program, but he wanted you to know that he's desperately sorry for what he did.''

She ground her teeth together. She knew that. Her father wasn't a bad man. Until he'd started abusing alcohol, he'd been one of the gentlest men alive. But, like all human beings, he had a breaking point which he reached when tragedy erupted into his life.

"He isn't a bad man," she said quietly. "Although I know it must have seemed like it."

"I've seen drunks before," Rey replied. "My brothers have gone on benders a time or two." He smiled faintly. "In fact, Leo holds the current record for damage at Shea's Bar, out on the Victoria road. He doesn't cut loose often, but when he does, people notice."

"He doesn't seem the sort of man who would do that," she remarked, surprised.

"We're all the sort of men who would do that, given the right provocation," he told her.

She smiled. "Do you get drunk and wreck bars?" she couldn't resist asking.

"I don't drink as a rule," he said simply. "A glass of wine rarely, nothing stronger. I don't like alcohol."

She smiled. "Neither do I."

He leaned back in his chair and studied her quietly. His hair was still faintly disheveled where her hands had caught in it when he was kissing her, and his lower lip was swollen from the pressure of her mouth. She knew she must look almost as bad. Her hand went unconsciously to her unruly hair.

"Take it down," he said abruptly.

"Wh...what?"

"Take your hair down," he said huskily. "I want to see it."

She'd just gotten her wild heart under control, and now

it was galloping all over again from that sultry tone, from the dark, intent caress of his eyes on her face.

"Listen, I work for you," she began with a tremor in her voice.

He got up from the chair and moved toward her with a lazy, almost arrogant stride. He drew her up in front of him and started pulling out hairpins. Her hair, unbound, fell in soft waves down her back, almost concealing one eye.

"It's hard to manage when it's down," she said self-consciously.

"I love long hair." He tangled his lean hands in it and coaxed her face up to his. He searched her eyes at point-blank range. "I've kissed girls years younger than you who knew even more than I do. Why are you still a novice?"

She swallowed hard. He was making her knees weak again. She couldn't quite get a whole breath of air into her lungs. Her hands rested on his chest lightly and she felt her heart choking her with its rapid beat as she stared into his narrowed, dark eyes.

"What?" she asked, barely having heard much less understood the question.

His hands were exploring the cool length of her hair with fascination. "You're not bad-looking, Meredith. Surely you've dated."

"Yes," she said, disconcerted. "But I'm old-fashioned."

Both eyebrows went up over a cynical smile. "That's a pitiful excuse in this day and age."

"Why?" she asked, her clear grey eyes staring up into his with no thought of subterfuge. "The whole reason for the women's movement is so that women can have the freedom to do as they please. I'm not promiscuous. Why should I need an excuse?"

He blinked. She made his question sound unreasonable. "I thought sexual liberation was the soul of the movement," he drawled.

"Being chaste is sexual liberation, in my book," she

replied. "You'd be amazed how many women in my graduating class practiced abstinence."

"In high school, I gather," he said absently, tracing the length of her hair with his hands.

She almost corrected him, but then, she really mustn't destroy the illusions he had about her as a domestic. "Yes. In high school."

He moved closer to her, his lean body a sensual provocation that made her breath catch. He laughed softly. "Care to test the hypothesis?" he murmured softly.

"I work for you," she repeated, playing for time.

"So?"

"So it's not wise to mix business..."

"...with pleasure?" He caught her waist and drew her close. "It's been a while since I found a woman so desirable," he whispered, bending to her mouth. "Experience bores me. You," he bit off against her soft lips, "are a challenge."

"Thank you, but I don't want to be," she whispered, trying to pull away.

He lifted his head and searched her eyes. "No curiosity about the great unknown?" he taunted.

"No desire to treat it as a sophisticated game," she corrected abruptly.

He hesitated, but only for an instant. His lean hands contracted and then released her. He went back to his chair and sat down. "Touché," he said with a curious glance. "All right, Meredith, I'll sit here and eat my sandwiches and we'll pretend that we're still strangers physically."

"Good idea," she approved. She reached down for her half-empty coffee cup and put it in the sink.

He was halfway through a sandwich when she excused herself and went to fluff up the pillows in the living room and put magazines and books back in their places. Leo had left things strewn about before he'd gone to the Brewsters'.

She was glad, because it gave her a valid reason not to sit next to Rey with her emotions in turmoil.

By the time she'd gone back to the kitchen, Rey had finished his sandwiches and coffee and was coming out the door.

"You're safe," he drawled. "I'm going to change and get to work in the study. Where's Leo?"

"Having supper at the Brewsters' house," she told him. "He said he'd be early."

"That means he'll be late," he mused. "Janie Brewster will have found twenty excuses to keep him talking to her father. She's one determined young lady, but Leo's equally determined. He doesn't want ties."

"Doesn't that sound familiar?" she murmured wickedly.

His eyes slid up and down her body in a silence that teemed with tension. "I never said I didn't want ties," he corrected. "I said I didn't want marriage. There's a difference."

"Don't look at me," she said carelessly. "I don't have time for relationships."

"Of course. All that cleaning must demand a lot of you," he said deliberately.

She flushed. He had no idea what her life was like on a daily basis, and she wanted very badly to tell him. But he was so almighty arrogant and condescending that he put her back up. She wasn't going to tell him a thing. He'd find out soon enough.

She put her hands on her hips and stared at him. "And what's wrong with being a housekeeper?" she demanded, going on the offensive. "Where would you and your brother be right now if there weren't women you could hire to bake and clean for you? I guess you'd have to get married then, or learn to cook, wouldn't you?"

He glared at her. "I could cook if I wanted to."

"You're the sort of man who makes a woman wish she

didn't have a culinary skill to her name," she said icily. "You are so 'lord of the manor-ish', Mr. Hart!"

"It isn't a manor," he pointed out. "They have those in England. We call this a ranch."

She glared at him.

He grinned. "You really do rise to the bait beautifully," he murmured, and something flashed in his dark eyes. "The sandwiches were good," he added.

She looked surprised. "Nothing but ham and a home-made sauce," she faltered.

"You do that a lot with food," he remarked gently. "I like the way you experiment with dishes. I even like the way you garnish the plates. You make things look appetizing."

She didn't realize that he'd even noticed. "I learned that from a dietician," she said without thinking. "If food is decorative, sometimes it makes up for bulk."

He smiled quizzically. "You can't decorate biscuits," he teased. "But you make really good ones."

"Thanks." She smiled back. "I'll tidy up the kitchen if you're through."

"I am. Don't stay up too late," he added and his eyes were suddenly bright with mischief. "You need plenty of rest so that you can make biscuits for breakfast!"

"Okay. I'll get an early night." She laughed and went on past him to the kitchen.

He stared after her for several long seconds with an expression that he was glad she didn't see. He liked the taste of her. That hadn't been wise, kissing her that way. He was going to have to make sure it didn't happen again. He didn't need complications.

Nothing was the same between Meredith and Rey after that day. They were aware of each other. It wasn't blatant, but she could feel tingling in her spine when Rey was in a room. It was instinctive. Her eyes followed him like puppies, and she flushed wildly when he caught her at it and gave her that amused, wordily glance.

Leo noticed, too, and it worried him that Rey was encouraging Meredith. He knew Rey too well to think he'd had a change of heart toward his bachelor status.

"You're leading her on," Leo accused his brother one evening when they were alone in the study with the door closed. "Why?"

Rey gave him a surprised glance. "You make it sound like a crime to flirt with her."

"In your case, it is," his brother said flatly. "You're a rounder. She isn't."

Rey shrugged. "She's not exactly off limits," he told his brother. "Not at her age."

"And what do you have in mind? Seduction?" Leo persisted irritably. "She's already been damaged enough by what happened with her father. The bruises are barely healed, and the mental scars are still there. Don't play games with her."

"Aren't you self-righteous all of a sudden?" Rey shot back angrily. "You've been stringing Janie Brewster along for weeks, and we both know you don't have any intention in hell of getting serious about her. All you want is first chance at that damned seed bull they're thinking of selling! Does she know?" he added maliciously.

Leo's eyes began to glitter. "Janie is a child," he said furiously. "I pick at her, and not because of any damned bull. I'm certainly not hell-bent on seduction!"

"She's not a child," Rey countered. "You're leading her down a blind alley, when you know full well she's in love with you."

Leo looked shocked. "She's not in love with me! Maybe she's got a crush. That's all!"

"You don't see the way she looks at you, do you?" Rey replied solemnly.

Leo cleared his throat. "We're talking about Meredith," he said firmly.

Rey's eyes narrowed. "Meredith is an adult."

"And she works for us," Leo went on relentlessly. "I'm not going to stand by and let you make an amusement of her."

"Jealous?" his brother taunted.

Leo was very still. "Is that the draw?" he asked softly. "Are we competing for a woman again?"

Rey's eyes flashed. "I would never have known about Carlie if you hadn't started propositioning her in front of me. Do you think I can forget that?"

"I keep hoping you will someday. She would have taken you for the ride of your life," Leo said quietly. "You're my brother. I couldn't stand by and do nothing."

Rey turned away with a muttered curse. Leo was right; he had saved him from even worse heartache, but the memory was still raw enough to hurt.

"Don't try to take it out on Meredith," Leo told him firmly. "She's had enough tragedy. Let her do her job."

Rey glanced at him over his shoulder. "I would, if she'd remember why she's here," he said venomously. "It's not my fault that every time I turn around, she's drooling over me! A saint could be tempted by a woman whose eyes worship him like that. I'm only human!"

"Don't raise your voice," Leo cautioned.

"Why? Do you think she's standing outside the door eavesdropping?" Rey drawled sarcastically. "What if she did hear me? It's the truth. She wants me. A blind man could see it."

"That's no reason to take advantage of her. She's not like your usual women."

"No, she's not. She has no ambition, no intellect. Besides that, she's so inexperienced, it's unreal. I never thought kissing a woman could be boring, until she came along," Rey added coldly, trying not to let Leo see how attracted he was to their housekeeper. ''She's so naive, it's nauseating.''

Outside the door, Meredith stood poised like a statue with a cup of coffee in a saucer shaking in her hands. She'd come to offer it to Rey, and overheard words that had never been meant for her ears. She fought tears as she turned around and went quickly and silently back down the hall to the kitchen.

Hearts couldn't really break, she told herself firmly, as she dabbed at the tears with a paper towel. She was just feeling the aftereffects of her devastating experience at home. It wasn't as if she was really drooling over Rey Hart.

She felt like sinking through the floor when she realized that she did spend an inordinate amount of time staring at him. He was handsome, sensuous, attractive. She liked looking at him. And maybe she was infatuated, a little. That didn't give him the right to say such horrible things about her.

If she hadn't been listening, she'd never have known about them in the first place. She'd have gone right ahead, mooning over him and having him know it and be amused by it. Her pride felt tattered. She'd never been one to wear her heart on her sleeve, but Rey had kissed her as if he enjoyed it, and she'd built dreams on those kisses. She realized now how truly naive it had been. The first man who paid her any attention in years, and she fell head over heels for him. Seen in that context, perhaps it wasn't surprising after all. She'd heard Leo accuse him of being a rounder, and she had to admit that his experience ran rings around hers. Apparently he was accustomed to playing sensual games with women. That was all those devastating kisses that had brought her to her knees had meant to him—just a game. And she'd taken it seriously!

Well, she told herself firmly, he needn't worry that she'd throw herself at his feet again. From now on, she was going to be the perfect employee, polite and courteous and eager to please—but she'd never stare at him longingly again. Thank God she'd overheard what he said to Leo. It had spared her a terrible humiliation. A little hurt now was far better than being wrung out emotionally down the road because she'd been ignorant of the facts. Wasn't she herself always telling people that the truth, however brutal, was always best in the long run? It was time to take her own advice.

When Rey and Leo came in to breakfast the next morning, she put bacon and eggs and biscuits on the table with a cool, professional smile.

Rey was oddly subdued. He didn't give her the arrogant scrutiny that had become force of habit in recent days. In fact, he didn't look at her at all. Leo kept up a pleasant conversation about the day's chores. They were moving some sick cattle into a pasture near the house so the vet could examine them, and stock was being shifted into closer quarters as well, within easier reach of the hay barn.

"I thought you had those big round bales of hay?" Meredith asked curiously.

"We do," Leo agreed. "But we still bale it the old-fashioned way and stack it in the barn. You lose some of the round bales through weathering by sun and rain. The hay that's kept dry in the barn has less deterioration and better nutrition."

"But you feed more than hay?"

Leo chuckled. He buttered a second biscuit. "You are sharp. Yes, we have a man who mixes feeds for better nutrition. No animal proteins, either," he added. "We're reactionaries when it comes to ranching. No artificial hormones, no pesticides, nothing except natural methods of pest control and growth. We're marketing our beef under the Hart Ranch label, as well, certifying it organic. We've already got several chain supermarkets carrying our product, and we've just moved onto the Internet to extend our distribution.''

"That's amazing," Meredith said with genuine interest. "It's like having custom beef," she added, nodding.

"It is custom beef," Leo told her. "We're capitalizing on the move toward healthier beef. Quick profit methods are going to fail producers in the long run, especially with the current attitude toward hormones and antibiotics and animal-product proteins for feed. We think that once organic beef catches on, the market will justify the added expense.''

"Word of mouth will take you far, too," Meredith said. "Hospitals teach nutrition these days, not only to patients but to the community. Tailored beef will find a market among consumers with heart problems, who'll pay the extra cost for healthier cuts of meat grown organically.''

Rey was listening. He finished his biscuit and poured himself another cup of coffee from the carafe on the table. "J.D. Langley pioneered that organic approach locally," he remarked. "He and the Tremayne boys got into terrific fights with other producers at seminars for a while. Then we saw the disasters overseas and suddenly everybody else was jumping on the bandwagon.''

"They'll be glad they did, I think," Meredith said.

"Which reminds me," Leo said, eyeing her. "Mrs. Lewis said her larder hadn't been opened since you came here. So…what are you making these biscuits with?''

She gave them a wary glance. "Light olive oil," she said slowly.

Rey gaped at his biscuit as if it had suddenly sprouted hair. "Olive oil?!" he gasped.

"Listen," she said quickly, aware of horrified stares, "olive oil is so healthy that people who live on a Mediterranean diet have only a fraction of the vascular problems we have in abundance in this country. The fat content is still there, but it's a vegetable fat, and it's actually good for you. Until I told you, you didn't even know you'd given up great gobs of animal fat in those biscuits!''

The brothers looked at each other. ''Well,'' Leo had to admit, ''they taste just as good as the others did.''

''That's true,'' Rey agreed reluctantly.

''And we're getting older,'' Leo continued. ''We don't want clogged arteries giving us heart attacks and strokes.''

''Or bypass surgery,'' Rey sighed.

''So I guess olive oil isn't so bad, after all,'' Leo concluded, with a grin at Meredith.

She grinned back. ''Thank goodness. I had visions of being tarred and feathered,'' she confessed.

''I'm not giving up butter, though,'' Rey told her firmly, dipping his knife into the tub next to the biscuit basket. ''Nothing tastes like real butter on a biscuit.''

Meredith didn't look at him. She couldn't confess that what he was eating was not butter, but rather a light margarine that actually lowered cholesterol levels. She only smiled and poured herself another cup of coffee.

Leo and Rey had started moving bulls into the lower pasture, where new forage grasses were thriving even in autumn, when a mangy old longhorn bull suddenly jerked his head and hooked Leo in the shoulder.

Leo yelled and threw a kick at him, but the aggravating animal was already trotting nonchalantly into the new pasture without a backward glance.

''How bad is it?'' Rey asked, leaving the cowboys to work the cattle alone while he looked at his brother's shoulder.

''Probably needs stitches,'' Leo said through his teeth. ''Drive me to the house and let me change shirts, then you can take me to Lou Coltrain.''

''Damned bull,'' Rey muttered as he put his brother into the ranch truck and took off home.

Meredith was sweeping off the back steps when they drove up. She gave Leo's bloodstained shirt a quick glance.

"Come on in here, let me have a look," she said gently.

Disconcerted, Leo let her remove the shirt from his shoulder and bathe the blood away with a clean cloth.

She probed around the edges of the cut and nodded. "You'll need stitches. Here. Hold this tight against the cut until you get to town."

"I need to change shirts," he began.

"You need to get to the doctor. Which one do you use?" she persisted, picking up the mobile phone she kept on the table.

"Dr. Lou Coltrain," he said.

"I'll phone and tell them you're on the way," she said firmly.

Rey gave her a curious glance, but he hustled Leo out the door and into the truck again.

When they got to the office, Dr. Lou Coltrain's nurse, Betty, came right out to meet them and guide them back into a cubicle.

Lou walked in, took a professional look at the cut, and grinned. "Stitches," she said. "How about a tetanus jab?"

Leo grimaced. "Well…"

She patted him on the shoulder that wasn't injured. "We'll have you fixed up and out of here in no time."

He sighed, glancing at his brother. "I hate shots."

Rey shrugged. "You'd hate tetanus more," he told Leo. "Besides," he added, "I hear she gives sugarless gum to the good patients."

Leo made a face at him.

When Leo was stitched up and given his tetanus shot, Rey drove him back to the house, where Meredith made him a cup of coffee and cut him a slice of cherry pie, making sure he had a cushion for his back in the straight chair at the table.

Rey glared at the special treatment his brother was getting. "Maybe I should get gored," he commented drolly.

Meredith stared at him, and she didn't smile. "You'd get a vinegar dressing and a cup of cold coffee," she said.

He glared at her, too. He felt as if he'd been put in the corner without supper. It wasn't a feeling he liked. He gave them both a hard look and went back out the door, smoldering with bad temper.

Six

"**I** shouldn't have said that," Meredith said wryly when Rey was gone. "I set him off again."

"It won't hurt him to have one woman who doesn't fall all over herself when he's around," Leo told her flatly. "Sometimes too much success can ruin a good man."

She toyed with her coffee cup. "Women like him, I guess," she said.

He gave her a quick glance that she didn't see before he started on his pie. "He's had girlfriends since he was in grammar school. But there was only one serious one. She turned out to be a real loser," he added quietly. "She soured him on women."

She sipped coffee. "You can't judge an entire sex by one woman," she pointed out.

"Well, we had our mother as an example, too," he continued. "She left Dad with five young boys and never looked back. We haven't been overawed with sterling examples of womanhood, although Simon and Corrigan and Cag have made good marriages in spite of that.''

She smiled absently as she looked at him. "I had a brother of my own," she said without thinking.

"Yes, I know," Leo replied, surprising her into silence. "His name was Michael Johns. He worked for Houston PD."

Her gasp was audible. "How...do you know about him?"

"Remember Colter Banks?"

"Yes. Colter was Mike's best friend."

"Well, Colter's our second cousin," he told her. "I knew Mike, too. I'm sorry."

She clenched one fist in her lap and tried not to give way to tears. "Do the others...know?"

"No, they don't," he replied. "They weren't that close to Colter, and they never met Mike. I haven't told them, and I'm not planning to."

She searched his dark eyes. "What else do you know about me, Leo?" she asked, because of the way he was watching her.

He shrugged. "Everything."

She let out a long breath. "And you haven't shared it with Rey."

"You wouldn't want me to," he murmured dryly. "He's having too much fun being condescending. When the time comes, he's got a few shocks coming, hasn't he?"

She laughed softly. "I hadn't meant to be cloak-and-daggerish. It's just that it still hurts too much to talk about," she said honestly.

"Colter told me the circumstances. It wasn't your fault," he replied. "Or your father's. I gather that he drinks because he feels responsible?"

She nodded. "We both dined out on 'what-if' just after it happened," she confessed. "I know that it probably wouldn't have made any difference, but you can't help wondering.''

"It doesn't do any good to torment yourself over things that are history," Leo said gently.

"I don't do it intentionally," she murmured.

"The first step was getting your father into treatment," he said. "Getting you out of your rut was the second. You don't have any memories to contend with here. I've noticed the difference in you just in the past week." He smiled. "You're changing already."

"I suppose so." She smiled back. "I've never even been on a ranch before. I could love it here. It's such a change of pace."

"When you're back to normal, we've got plenty of opportunity around here for your sort of job," he pointed out.

She chuckled. "Don't rush me. It's far too soon to think about leaving Houston." She didn't add that she didn't want to be that close to Rey, considering his opinion of her at the moment. "I've only been down here a week."

"Okay. I'll let it drop, for now." He leaned back in his chair and winced, favoring the arm he'd had stitched. "Damned bull," he muttered.

"Did they give you something for the pain?"

"No, and I didn't ask for anything. I have over-the-counter painkillers if it gets really bad. So far, it hasn't."

"You know, of course, that statistically farm and ranch work have the highest ratio of accidents," she said.

"Any job can be dangerous," he said easily.

She pursed her lips and lifted her coffee cup to them. "Your brother's a walking job hazard," she said thoughtfully.

"Oh? In what way, exactly?" he asked.

She wouldn't have touched that line with a pole. She laughed. "He's abrasive. I don't think he wants me here."

"I've noticed his attitude. I hope you haven't let it get to you?"

"I haven't. Anyway, he'll mellow one of these days," she said.

"He could use some mellowing. He's a disillusioned man."

She smoothed the lip of the cup. "Did he love her very much?"

He knew she was talking about Carlie. He sighed. "He thought he did. His pride suffered more than his heart." He hesitated. "I didn't help matters. I made a play for her deliberately, to show him what she was. That was a miscalculation. A bad one. He's never forgiven me for it. Now, if I pay any attention to a woman, he tries to compete with me…"

She noticed the way his voice trailed off, and she averted her eyes. "I get the picture," she said.

"It's not like that, not with you," he began.

She forced a smile. "He's not interested in me," she said bluntly. "And just in case you're worried that I might be falling all over him, there's no danger of that, either. I was outside the door when he was talking to you. I wasn't eavesdropping, but he was speaking rather loudly. I heard what he said. I'd have to be certifiable to lose my heart over a man like that."

He grimaced as he read the faint pain that lingered in her eyes. "I wouldn't have had you hear what he said for the world," he said deeply.

She managed a smile. "It's just as well. It will keep me from taking him seriously. Besides, I'm not really down here looking for a soul mate."

"Just as well, because Rey isn't any woman's idea of the perfect partner, not the way he is right now. I love him dearly, but I can afford to. It's another story for any woman who loses her heart to him." He studied her warily. "Just don't let him play you for a fool."

"I wouldn't dream of it," she said. "Even if I got the chance."

He nodded. He finished his pie and coffee and got to his feet. "I'd better change and get back to work. Thanks for running interference, by the way. You're a cool head in an emergency," he remarked with a smile.

"I've had lots of practice," she said modestly and grinned. "But try to stay away from horned things for a while."

"Especially my brother, the minor devil," he said, tongue-in-cheek, and grinned back when she got the reference and started laughing.

After Leo went back to work, Meredith went out to gather eggs. It seemed very straightforward. You walked into the henhouse, reached in the nest, and pulled out a dozen or so big brown eggs, some still warm from the chicken's feathered body.

But that wasn't what happened. She paused just inside the henhouse to let her eyes adjust to the reduced light, and when she moved toward the row of straw-laced nests, she saw something wrapped around one nest that wasn't feathered. It had scales and a flickering long tongue. It peered at her through the darkness and tightened its coils around its prey, three big brown eggs.

Meredith, a city girl with very little experience of scaly things, did something predictable. She screamed, threw the basket in the general direction of the snake, and left skid marks getting out of the fenced lot.

Annie Lewis, who was doing the laundry, came to the back door as fast as her arthritis would allow, to see what all the commotion was about.

"There's a...big black and white *snnnnnakkkkke*...in there!" Meredith screamed, shaking all over from the close encounter.

"After the eggs, I reckon," Annie said with a sigh. She wiped her hands on her apron. "Let me get a stick and I'll deal with it."

"You can't go in there alone with the horrible thing and try to kill it! It must be five feet long!"

"It's a king snake, not a rattler," Annie said gently, recognizing the description. "And I'm not planning to kill it. I'm going to get it on a stick and put in the barn. It can eat its fill of rats and poisonous snakes and do some good out there."

"You aren't going to kill it?" Meredith exclaimed, horrified.

"It's a king snake, dear," came the gentle reply. "We don't like to kill them. They're very useful. They eat rattlesnakes, you know."

"I didn't know." Meredith shivered again. "I've never seen a snake except in a zoo, and it was a python."

"You'll see lots of them out here in the country. Just remember that if one rattles at you, it means business and it will strike. Rattlesnakes are venomous."

Meredith looked around as if she expected to be mobbed just at the mention of them.

"You can finish the washing," Annie said, trying not to grin. "I'll take care of the snake."

"Please be careful!"

"I will. After all, you get used to things like..."

Rey drove up and stopped the truck just short of the two women, exiting it with his usual graceful speed.

"What's going on?" he asked as he pulled a box of assorted bovine medicines out of the boot of the truck.

"There's a snake in the henhouse!" Meredith exclaimed.

He stopped with the supplies in his arms and stared at her curiously. "So?" he asked.

"I'm just going to move it for her, Rey," Mrs. Lewis said with a grin. "It sounds like a king snake. I thought I'd put him in the barn."

"I'll get him for you." He put the box on the hood of the truck. "Scared of snakes, are you?" he scoffed.

"I'd never seen one until a few minutes ago," she said

huffily, and flushed. He was looking at her as if she were a child.

"There's a first time for everything," he said, and his eyes made a very explicit remark as they lingered on her breasts.

She gave him a glare hot enough to fry bacon, which he ignored. He walked right into the chicken lot and, then, into the henhouse.

Barely a minute later, he came back out with the snake coiled around one arm, its neck gently held in his other hand.

"Would you look at this, it's Bandit!" he exclaimed, showing it to a fascinated Mrs. Lewis. "See the scar on his back where he got caught in the corn sheller that time?"

"So it is!" she said. "Hello, old fella!" She actually petted the vile thing under the chin.

"How can you touch that thing?!" Meredith groaned. "It's a snake!"

Mrs. Lewis glanced at Rey. "Reckon we should tell her that he used to live in the house?"

"Probably not," Rey suggested, aware of her white face. "I'll just stick him up in the loft. Come on, Bandit, I'll put you in a safe place."

Meredith was holding both chill-bump laden arms with her hands and shivering.

"There, there," Annie said gently. "He wouldn't bite you unless you provoked him. He's very gentle."

"If you say so."

"I do. Now you go back in there and get the eggs. Don't let Rey see how frightened you are. Trust me, he'll take advantage of it. You'll find rubber snakes in the refrigerator, the blender, the washer..."

"No!" Meredith exclaimed, horrified.

"Just grit your teeth and go back in the henhouse," Annie suggested. "Quick, before he comes back out."

Meredith took a quick breath and gave Annie a miserable glance, but she did as she was told.

Her skin crawled when she had to pick up the basket and gather the eggs, especially the ones the snake had been curled around. Now, every time she went to the henhouse, she'd be shivering with apprehension.

You've looked at gunshot wounds, accident victims, every sort of horror known to human eyes, she told herself firmly. The snake wasn't even lacerated! So get it done and move on.

She did, walking back out into the sunlight with a full basket of eggs and a forced look of composure on her soft face.

Rey was waiting for her, leaning against the bumper of the truck with his arms crossed and his hat pulled low over his eyes.

She didn't dare look at him for long. In that indolent pose, his lean, muscular body was shown to its very best advantage. It made her tingle to think how it had felt to be held against every inch of that formidable frame, to be kissed by that long, hard mouth.

"You get thrown, you get right back on the horse," he said with approval. "I'm proud of you, Meredith. It would be hard for even a ranch-born girl to go back into a henhouse where a snake had been lurking."

She took a slow breath. "We don't face things by running away from them, I guess," she agreed.

His eyes narrowed under the wide brim of the hat. "What are you running away from, Meredith? What is your father running away from?"

She clutched the basket to her chest. "That's nothing that you need to concern yourself with," she said with quiet dignity.

"You work for me," he replied.

"Not for long," she pointed out. "In another week or so, I'll be a memory."

"Will you?" He lurched away from the bumper and went to stand just in front of her, a tall and sensual threat. His fingers touched her soft mouth lightly. "Those bruises still look pretty fresh," he pointed out. "And you did ask for a month's leave, or so you said. Did you?"

She grimaced. "Well, yes, but I don't have to stay here all that time."

"I think you do," he returned. He bent and drew his mouth slowly over hers, a whisper of a contact that made her breath catch. He smiled with faint arrogance as he stood up again. "Anything could happen," he drawled. "You might like ranch life."

"I don't like snakes already."

"That was a fluke. They're generally hibernating by November, but it's been unseasonably warm. Spring is generally when you have to watch where you put your hands. But you don't need to worry. I'll protect you from snakes. And other perils."

"Who'll protect me from you?" she asked huskily.

He raised any eyebrow. "Why would you need protection?" he asked. "You're well over the age of consent."

"I've lived a very sheltered life," she said flatly.

He pursed his lips as he studied her, examining the statement. "Maybe it's time you walked out of the cocoon."

"I'm not in the market for an affair."

"Neither am I." He smiled slowly. "But if you worked at it, you might change my mind."

"I don't think so," she said. Her eyes were cool as they met his. "I wouldn't want you to think I was 'drooling' over you," she added deliberately.

His face changed. He knew immediately that she'd overheard what he'd said to Leo. He was sorry, because it wasn't true. He'd been desperate to throw Leo off the track. He didn't want his brother to know how attracted he was to her.

"Eavesdroppers never hear anything good about themselves, don't they say?" he asked quietly.

"Never," she agreed. "Now, if you'll excuse me, I'll go wash the eggs."

"I said something else that you'll remember with sordid ease," he murmured as she started past him. He caught her by the shoulder and tugged her close, bending to drag his mouth roughly across hers. "But I didn't mean that, either," he whispered against her parted lips. "Your innocence makes my head spin. I lay awake at night thinking of all sorts of delicious ways to relieve you of it."

"You'd be lucky!" she exclaimed, shocked.

He laughed softly as he let her go. "So would you," he drawled. "I've been called 'sensual hell' in bed, and I can assure you it wasn't meant to be a derogatory remark."

"Rey Hart!" she burst out.

"But why take anyone else's word for it?" he teased. "I'll be glad to let you see for yourself, anytime you like."

"If you think...I have never...of all the...!"

"Yes, it does tend to make women flustered when I mention what a great lover I am," he said with a wicked grin.

She couldn't get one coherent sentence out. She stomped her foot hard, turned around, and stormed into the kitchen, almost knocking herself down with the door in the process. It didn't help that Rey stood out there laughing like a predator.

If she expected Rey to be apologetic about what he'd said, she was doomed to disappointment. He watched her with narrow, assessing eyes as she went about her household duties. He didn't harass her, or monopolize her. He just watched. The scrutiny made her so nervous that she fumbled constantly. Her heart ran wild at the attention from those dark, steady eyes.

"Why don't you want to do something else besides keep house?" Rey asked her one evening when she was putting supper on the table. Leo, as usual, was late getting in. Rey had volunteered to set the table while she fixed Mexican corn bread and chili.

"Keeping house has less stress than most outside jobs," she said, not looking at him.

"It pays lousy wages," he continued, "and you could get into a lot of trouble in some households, with men who'd see you as fair game."

"Do you see me that way?" she asked, wide-eyed.

He glowered at her. "No, I don't. The point is, some other man might. It isn't a safe career. In a profession, there are more laws to protect you."

"Most professional people have degrees and such. Besides, I'm too old."

"You're never too old to go back to school," he replied.

She shrugged. "Besides, I like cooking and cleaning."

He eyed her curiously. "You're very good at handling injured people," he said suddenly. "And you're remarkably calm in an emergency."

"It's good practice for when I have kids," she said.

He drew in a short breath. "You like being mysterious, don't you?"

"While it lasts, it's fun," she agreed.

His eyes narrowed. "What dark secrets are you keeping, Meredith?" he asked quietly.

"None that should bother you, even if you found them out," she assured him. She smiled at him from the stove. "Meanwhile, you're getting fresh biscuits every day."

"Yes, we are," he had to agree. "And you're a good cook. But I don't like mysteries."

She pursed her lips and gave him a teasing glance over her shoulder. "Too bad."

He put the last place setting on the table and sat down at his place, just staring at her, without speaking. "You know," he said after a minute, frowning, "there's something familiar about your last name. I can't quite place it, but I know I've heard it somewhere.''

That wasn't good, she thought. He might remember Leo talking about her brother. She didn't want to have to face the past, not just yet, when she was still broken and bruised and uncomfortable. When she was back on her feet and well again, there would be time to come to grips with it once and for all—as her poor father was already doing.

''Think so?'' she asked with forced nonchalance.

He shrugged. ''Well, it may come back to me one day.''

Fortunately Leo came in and stopped his train of thought. Meredith put supper on the table and sat down to eat it with the brothers.

The next morning, Rey came out to the kitchen with a bright silver metal gun case. He set it down beside the counter, out of the way, before he started eating his breakfast.

''Going hunting?'' Meredith asked impishly.

He gave her a wary glance. ''Skeet shooting,'' he corrected. ''The season's over, but I practice year-round.''

''He won two medals at the World championships in San Antonio, this year,'' Leo told her with a grin. ''He's an 'A' class shooter.''

''Which gauge?'' she asked without thinking.

Rey's face became suspicious. ''All of them. What do you know about shotguns?''

''I used to skeet-shoot,'' she volunteered. ''My brother taught me how to handle a shotgun, and then he got me into competition shooting. I wasn't able to keep it up after I grad...after high school,'' she improvised quickly. She didn't dare tell him she gave it up after she finished college. That would be giving away far too much.

He watched her sip coffee. ''You can shoot, can you?'' he asked, looking as if he were humoring her. He didn't seem to believe what she claimed.

"Yes, I can," she said deliberately.

He smiled. "Like to come down to the range with me?" he asked. "I've got a nice little .28 gauge I can bring along for you."

By offering her his lowest caliber shotgun, he was assuming that she couldn't handle anything heavier.

"What's in the case?" she asked.

"My twelve gauge," he said.

She gave him a speaking glance. "I'll just shoot that, if you don't mind sharing it. Uh, it doesn't have a kick or anything…?" she added, and had to bite her tongue to keep from grinning at her innocent pose.

He cleared his throat. He didn't dare look at Leo. "No," he said carelessly. "Of course it doesn't have a kick."

In truth, it would kick worse than any other of the four gauges, but Rey was planning to call her bluff. She was putting on an act for his benefit. He was going to make her sorry she tried it.

"Then I'll be just fine with that gun," she said. "More apple butter?" She offered him an open jar and spoon.

"Thanks," he replied smugly, accepting the jar. He put it down and buttered another biscuit before he spooned the apple butter into it. "Don't mind if I do. Leo, want to come along?" he asked his brother.

Leo was also trying not to grin. "I think I will, this time," he told his brother. This was one shooting contest he wasn't about to miss. He knew that Mike Johns was a champion shooter. If he'd been the one who taught his sister, Meredith would shock Rey speechless when she got that shotgun in her arms. He was going along. He didn't want to miss the fun.

"The more the merrier, I always say," Rey chuckled.

"Funny thing, that's just what I was thinking," Leo replied, tongue-in-cheek.

Meredith didn't say another word. She finished her breakfast, waited until they finished theirs, and put the dishes in the dishwasher. Then she dressed in jeans, boots, and a long-sleeved flannel shirt with a down-filled vest and a bib cap, and went off to let Rey show her how to shoot a shotgun.

The target range was unusually busy for a lazy Friday afternoon in November. It was a cool day, with a nice nip in the air. Meredith felt good in the down vest. It was one she'd often worn when she went to the firing range with Mike in cold weather. Coats were cumbersome and often got in the way of a good, quick aim.

Rey and Leo stopped to pass the time of day with two elderly shooters, both of whom gave Meredith a warm welcome.

"This is Jack, and that's Billy Joe," Rey introduced the white-haired men, one of whom was tall and spare, the other overweight and short. The short one had walked briskly the short distance from the red pickup truck parked at the clubhouse, and he was out of breath already. "We all go to district, state and national shoots as a team from our club."

"But we get honorable mention, and Rey wins the medals," Billy Joe, the shorter man, chuckled, still trying to catch his breath. "We don't mind. We're just happy that somebody from our club breaks records!"

"Amen to that," Jack agreed, smiling.

"All right, let's get to shooting," Billy Joe said, turning back to his truck. "Stay where you are, Jack. I'll bring your gun, too!"

He turned back toward the truck, rushing and still breathless. Meredith frowned. His cheeks were unnaturally pink, and it wasn't that cold. His complexion was almost white. He was sweating. She knew the symptoms. She'd seen them all too often.

"You might go with him," Meredith said abruptly, interrupting Jack's banter with Rey.

"Excuse me?" Jack asked.

Just at that moment, Billy Joe stopped, stood very still for a minute, and then buckled and fell forward into a crumpled heap at the door of his truck.

Meredith took off at a dead run. "Somebody get me a cell phone!" she called as she ran.

Leo fumbled his out of the holder on his belt and passed it to her as she knelt beside Billy Joe.

"Get his feet elevated. Find something to cover him with," she shot at the other men. She was dialing while she spoke. She loosened the man's shirt, propping the phone against her ear—the worst way to hold it, but there was no other way at the moment—and felt down Billy Joe's chest for his diaphragm. "Get his wallet and read me his weight and age from his driver's license," she added with a sharp glance in Leo's direction.

Leo dug out the wallet and started calling out information, while Rey and Jack stood beside the fallen man and watched with silent concern.

"I want the resident on duty in the emergency room, stat," she said. "This is Meredith Johns. I have a patient, sixty years of age, one hundred and eighty pounds, who collapsed without warning. Early signs indicate a possible myocardial infarction. Pulse is thready," she murmured, checking the second hand of her watch as she took his pulse with her fingertips, "forty beats a minute, breathing shallow and labored, grey complexion, profuse sweating. I need EMTs en route, I am initiating cardiopulmonary resuscitation now."

There was a long pause, and a male voice came over the line. With her voice calm and steady, Meredith gave the information again, and then handed the phone to Leo as she bent over the elderly man and did the spaced compressions over his breastbone, followed by mouth-to-mouth breathing.

Rey was watching, spellbound at her proficiency, at the

easy and quite professional manner in which she'd taken charge of a life-or-death emergency. Within five minutes, the ambulance was screaming up the graveled road that led to the Jacobsville Gun Club, and Billy Joe was holding his own.

The EMTs listened to Meredith's terse summary of events as they called the same resident Meredith had been talking to.

"Doc says to give you a pat on the back," the female EMT grinned at Meredith as they loaded Billy Joe onto the ambulance. "You sure knew what to do."

"Yes," Rey agreed, finding his tongue at last. "You've obviously had first-aid training."

He probably meant it as praise, but it hit Meredith in the gut. She glared at him. "What I've had," she emphasized, "is five years of college. I have a master's degree in nursing science, and I'm a card-carrying nurse practitioner!"

Seven

Rey stared at his new cook as if she'd suddenly sprouted feathers on her head. His summation of her abilities was suddenly smoke. She was someone he didn't even know. She was a health care professional, not a flighty cook, and certainly not the sort of woman to streetwalk as a sideline.

She nodded solemnly. "I figured it would come as a shock," she told him. She turned her attention back to the EMTs. "Thanks for being so prompt. Think he'll be okay?"

The female EMT smiled. "I think so. His heartbeat's stronger, his breathing is regular, and he's regaining consciousness. Good job!"

She grinned. "You, too."

They waved and took off, lights flashing, but without turning on the sirens.

"Why aren't the sirens going?" Rey wanted to know. "He's not out of danger yet, surely?"

"They don't like to run the sirens unless they have to,"

Meredith told him. "Some people actually run off the road and wreck their cars because the sirens rattle them. They use the lights, but they only turn on the sirens if they hit heavy traffic and have to force their way through it. Those EMTs," she added with a smile, "they're the real heroes and heroines. They do the hardest job of all."

"You saved Billy Joe's life," Jack said huskily, shaking her hand hard. "He's the best friend I got. Thank you."

She smiled gently and returned the handshake. "It goes with the job description. Don't try to keep up with the ambulance," she cautioned when he went toward Billy Joe's truck, which still had the key in the ignition. The two men had come together.

"I'll be careful," the older man promised.

"Whew!" Leo let out the breath he'd almost been holding, and put up his cell phone. "You're one cool lady under fire, Meredith."

She smiled sadly. "I've had to be," she replied. She glanced at Rey, who looked cold and angry as it occurred to him, belatedly, that she'd played him for a fool. "I can see what you're thinking, but I didn't actually lie to you. You never asked me exactly what I did for a living. Of course, you thought you already knew," she added with faint sarcasm.

He didn't reply. He gave her a long, contemptuous look and turned away. "I've lost my taste for practice," he said quietly. "I want to go on to the hospital and see about Billy Joe."

"Me, too," Leo added. "Meredith...?"

"I'll go along," she said. "I'd like to meet that resident I spoke with. He's very good."

Rey glanced toward her. "You'll get along. He keeps secrets, too," he said bitterly, and got behind the wheel.

Leo made a face at Meredith, opening the third door of the big double cabbed truck so that she could sit in back.

He put the gun cases in the boot, in a locked area, and climbed in beside Rey.

The resident turned out to be a former mercenary named Micah Steele. He was married to a local girl, and he'd gone back to school to finish his course of study for his medical license.

"I couldn't very well carry a wife and child around the jungles with me," Micah told her with a grin. He was tall and big, and not at all bad-looking. She could picture him with a rifle in one arm. But now, in a white lab coat with a stethoscope thrown carelessly around his neck, he seemed equally at home.

"When's Callie due?" Leo asked.

"Any minute," he said, tongue-in-cheek. "Can't you see me shaking? I'm the soul of self-confidence around here, but one little pregnant woman makes me a basket case!"

"Callie's quite a girl," Rey agreed, smiling at the big man.

Micah gave him a look. "Yes, and isn't it lucky for me that you hardly ever went into her boss Kemp's office for legal advice, while she was still single?"

Rey pursed his lips. "Kemp eats scorpions for breakfast, I hear. I like my lawyers less caustic."

"Last I heard, the local bar association had you down as a contagious plague and was warning its members to avoid you at all costs," Micah replied wickedly.

"I never hit any local lawyers." Rey looked uncomfortable. "It was that Victoria lawyer, Matherson," he muttered. "And I didn't even hit him that hard. Hell, he's lucky I wasn't sober at the time! Otherwise, he'd have had twice the number of stitches!"

Meredith listened to the repartee with wide, fascinated eyes, but Rey wouldn't meet her eyes and Micah, too, cleared his throat and didn't pursue the subject.

"Matherson took a client who accused us of assault,"

Leo volunteered. "Cag had hit him, several times, after he got drunk and assaulted Tess, who's now Cag's wife. But the bounder swore that he was the injured party, that we falsely accused him and all took turns pounding him. He convinced a jury to award him damages. Not a lot of money," Leo added solemnly, "but the principle was what set Rey off. He was in a bad mood already and he had a few too many drinks at Shea's Bar, out on the Victoria road. To make a long story short," he added with a chuckle, "Matherson was having a quiet beer when Rey accused him of handling the ex-employee's case for spite because he lost an argument with us over Tess when he was handling her inheritance. Matherson took exception to Rey's remarks, and the two of them set about wrecking the pretty stained-glass window that used to overlook the parking lot."

"Used to?" Meredith fished, sensing something ominous.

"Yes, well, Matherson made a rather large hole in it when Rey helped him into the parking lot the hard way," Leo concluded.

Micah Steele looked as if it was killing him not to burst out laughing.

"He," Leo jerked his thumb toward Steele, "had to remove quite a number of glass particles from Matherson's rear end. *And* we got sued again, for that!"

"But the jury, after hearing Kemp's masterful summation of our grievances," Rey interrupted, "decided that Matherson was only entitled to the cost of the repair job on his butt. Shea had insurance that replaced the stained-glass window with one of comparable age and exclusivity." Rey smiled smugly. "And the judge said that if she'd been sitting on the first case, the rat Matherson was representing would have gotten a jail sentence."

Leo chuckled. "Only because Kemp put Tess on the stand and had her testify about what really happened the night Matherson's client took her on a date. The jury felt that Rey was justifiably incensed by the former verdict.'' He glanced at Meredith wryly.

''Yes, but I understand that Shea's two bouncers meet Rey at the door these days and won't let him in if he's not smiling,'' Micah contributed.

Rey shrugged. ''I never get drunk anymore. I've learned to handle aggression in a nonphysical manner.''

The other two men actually walked down the hall. Meredith noticed their shoulders vibrating.

Rey took a step toward Meredith, half irritated by the character assassination job his brother and Micah Steele had just done on him, and even more put out by Meredith's unmasking.

''You knew I had no idea about your education,'' Rey accused Meredith. ''Why didn't you say something at the outset, when Leo first went to the hospital?'' he demanded in a low, deep tone. ''I may have jumped to conclusions, but you provided the springs, didn't you?''

She grimaced. ''I guess so. But it was only a little jump from telling you about my job to talking about the reason Daddy started drinking. It's…still very fresh in my mind,'' she added huskily. ''It's only been six months. The memories are—'' she swallowed and looked away ''—bad.''

Unexpectedly he reached out and caught her fingers in his, tugging her closer. The hall was deserted. In the background there were muted bell-tones and announcements and the sound of lunch trays being distributed. ''Tell me,'' he said gently.

She bit her lower lip hard and lifted her tormented eyes to his curious ones. ''Not…yet,'' she whispered tightly. ''One day, but…not yet. I can't.''

''Okay,'' he said after a minute. ''But I'd like to know how you learned to shoot.''

''My brother, Mike, taught me,'' she said reluctantly, staring at his broad chest. She wanted to lay her head on

it and cry out her pain. There hadn't been anyone to hold
her, not when it happened, not afterward. Her father with-
drew into his own mind and started drinking to excess at
once. Her job was all that had kept Meredith sane. She
hadn't been able to let out her grief in any normal way.

Rey's mind was working overtime. He stared down at
her, still holding her fingers entwined tightly with his own,
and he frowned as bits and pieces of memory began fitting
themselves together.

"Mike. Mike Johns." His eyes narrowed. "Our cousin
Colter's best friend, and one of Leo's acquaintances. He
was killed...!"

She tried to tug her fingers away. He wouldn't let her.
He pulled her into his arms, holding her there even when
she struggled. But a few seconds of resistance were all she
had. She laid her flushed cheek against his broad chest and
let the tears flow.

Rey's arms contracted roughly. He smoothed his hand
over her nape, caressing, soothing. "There was a bank rob-
bery in Houston," he recalled quietly. "Mike was a cop.
He was at the bank with your mother. It was Saturday. He
was off duty, but he had his service revolver under his
jacket." His arms tightened as her sobs grew painful to
hear. "He drew and fired automatically, and one of the
robbers sprayed fire from one of those damned little automatic rifles in his general direction. He and your mother
died instantly..."

Meredith's fingers dug into his wide back. He rocked her,
barely aware of curious glances from passersby.

"Both men were caught. You don't kill a cop and get
away with it in Texas," he added softly. "They were ar-
raigned and treated to a speedy trial just a month ago. You
and your father testified. That was when your father really
went off the deep end, wasn't it, when he had to see the
autopsy photos..."

Micah and Leo came back down the hall, frowning when

they saw the condition Meredith was in. Even as they watched, her eyes rolled back and she would have fallen to the floor except for Rey's strong arms lifting her.

Later, she wouldn't recall much except that she was hustled into a cubicle and revived. But when she started sobbing hysterically, they'd given her a shot of something that put her out like a light. She came to back at the ranch, in her own little garage apartment.

She opened her eyes, and there was Rey, sitting by the bed, still wearing the same jeans and shirt and boots he'd worn to the shooting range. Meredith was aware of the bedspread covering her up to her waist. Her boots were off, but she was also wearing the same clothes she'd started out in that morning.

"What time is it?" she asked in a husky, slightly disoriented tone.

"Five hours past the time you flaked out on me," he said, smiling gently. "Micah knocked you out. He thought some sleep might help." The smile faded into quiet concern. "You don't sleep much, do you, Meredith?" he asked surprisingly.

She sighed, brushed back her disheveled blond hair, and shook her head. "When I go to sleep, I have nightmares. I wake up in a cold sweat, and I see them, lying there on the floor, just the way they looked in those vivid crime scene photos." She closed her eyes and shivered. "People look so fragile like that, they look like big dolls, sprawled in pitiful disarray on the floor. Everybody stares at them..."

He brushed back her hair with a lean, gentle hand. "They got the guys who did it," he reminded her. "Including the trigger man. He'll serve life without any hope of parole. He'll pay for it."

Her pale eyes were tormented as they met his. "Yes, but it won't bring them back, will it?" she asked. "And do you know why they said they did it? For a bet. For a stupid bet, they killed two innocent people!"

"They also ruined their own lives," he reminded her, "and the lives of their own families."

She looked at him blankly, scowling.

"Don't you ever think about that?" he asked softly. "Criminals have families, too. Most of them have loving, decent parents who took care of them and disciplined them and blame themselves for what their children do. It must be pure hell, to have your child kill someone, and feel responsible for it."

"I haven't considered that," she admitted.

He continued. "When I was in high school, one of my best friends was arrested for murder. He killed the old man next door in the process of stealing his wallet. He wanted to buy his girl a diamond necklace she liked, and he didn't have any money. He figured the man was old and didn't need money anyway, so he might as well take it. He was sorry about it, but he never figured on killing the man or getting caught."

"Was he a good friend?" she asked.

He looked at their linked fingers. He nodded. "We were pals since grammar school. He wasn't quite as bright as some of the other boys, but he had a gentle nature. Or so we thought." He met her eyes. "His mom and dad always had a houseful of other peoples' kids. They were everybody's mom and dad. It shattered them when Joey went to prison. Even the children of the old man felt sorry for them."

"Funny," she mused. "I never even thought of how it would feel to have a child or a parent or a sibling who broke the law in some terrible way." She met his eyes. "I guess I'd feel guilty, too."

"Most kids are raised right. But some of them have a wild streak that nobody can tame, others have poor impulse control. Many are handicapped. Nobody goes to jail because he wants to."

"I never thought of you as a sensitive man," she blurted out, and then flushed at the insult.

His eyebrows lifted. "Who, me? I stop to pick worms out of the highway so my tires won't bruise their little bodies, and you think I'm insensitive?"

It took a minute for the words to make sense, and then she burst out laughing.

"That's better," he said. He smiled and squeezed her fingers. "You're going to be okay. You've had a lot of traumatic experiences just lately. No wonder you caved in."

"Lucky for you," she shot back.

"Me? Why?"

"Because if we'd unpacked those shotguns, I'd have destroyed your ego," she said with a smug smile. "At Mike's gun club, they used to call me 'dead-eye.'"

"Oh, they did, did they?" he challenged. "Well, we'll see about that when you step up to my gun range."

She studied his lean face. He wasn't handsome, but he had strong, stubborn features. He was familiar to her now, almost necessary. She thought about going back to Houston with real panic.

He touched her cheek where the bruises were a mixture of purple and yellow, much less vivid now. "He really knocked you around," he said, and his face hardened visibly. "I don't care if a man is drunk, there's no excuse for hitting a woman."

"Shades of primitive man," she chided with a smile.

"Women are the cradles of life," he said simply. "What sort of man tries to break a cradle?"

"You have a unique way of putting things."

"We had Spanish ancestors," he told her. "They were old-world men, conquerors, adventurers. One of them made his way to Texas and was given a huge tract of land under a Spanish land grant, for services to the crown of Spain."

He noticed a start of surprise on her face. "Do you know the legend of the Cid?"

"Yes!" she exclaimed. "He was a great Spanish hero. Cid is for the Arabic 'Sidi' which means Lord."

"Well, our ancestor wasn't El Cid," he said on a chuckle. "But he fought his way through hostile neighbors to claim his land, and he held it as long as he lived. Our family still holds it, through our late uncle, who left us this ranch."

"This is the original grant?" she exclaimed.

He nodded. "It isn't nearly as big as it was a couple of hundred years ago, but it's no weekend farm, either. Didn't you notice the antique silver service in the dining room?"

"Yes, I've been afraid to touch it. It looks very old."

He smiled. "It came from Madrid. It's over two hundred years old."

"An heirloom!" she breathed.

"Yes. Like the ranch itself." He tilted his head and studied her for a long time. "Now I understand. Your father wasn't violent until the killer's trial, was he?"

"No, he wasn't." She looked down at Rey's big, warm hand wrapped around her own. It made her feel safe. "He told Mike to drive Mama to the bank," she added reluctantly. "He had papers to grade. He couldn't spare the time, he said, and he snapped at her when she protested that Mike was spending his day off, carting her all over Houston." She glanced at him. "I was called in to work at a clinic my boss holds in the Hispanic community every Saturday. There's a regular nurse, but she was at home with a sick child. I went to stand in for her." Her eyes fell to his broad chest. "I could have asked someone to go in my place. I didn't. So he and I both have our guilt."

"Because you lived and they didn't," Rey said bluntly.

She gasped. "No, that's not true!"

"It is true." His black eyes held hers relentlessly. "The same thing happens to people who survive airplane crashes,

automobile wrecks, sinking ships. It's a normal, human reaction to surviving when other people don't. It's worse
when the victims include close relatives or friends.''

"Where did you learn that?" she asked.

"From Janie Brewster," he said.

She frowned. "That name sounds familiar."

"We've mentioned her to you. She's the daughter of a
neighboring cattleman," he related. "She got her associate
degree in psychology from our community college, and
now she's studying it in Houston," he added with a grin.
"She's almost twenty. They let her take college courses
while she was still in high school, so she's ahead."

"Oh."

"She's not hard on the eyes, either," he murmured,
avoiding her eyes. "She and her father live alone. Leo and
I have a standing dinner invitation, any time we care to
show up."

She started to say "oh" again, and realized how juvenile
she was behaving. She straightened her shoulders against
the pillow that was propping her up, and tugged at the hand
Rey still held. "Then if she can bake biscuits, you're saved
when I leave, aren't you?" she asked coolly.

"Well, she can't exactly bake stuff," Rey had to admit.

"Why?"

"She has no sense of time. She sets the timer and it goes
off, and she never hears it. So the chicken bounces, the
heat-and-serve rolls usually come out black, and I won't
even mention what happens to vegetables she tries to cook
on *top* of the stove." He gave her a sad look. "She did try
to make us a pan of biscuits once." He actually shuddered.

"Not a successful try?" she fished.

"We had to take the damned things home, or her father
would never have let us near the Salers heifers he was
offering for sale." He glanced at her. "Leo just bought us
a big Salers bull, and we needed purebred heifers to breed
to him. Purebred breeding stock brings a big price, espe-

cially if you show cattle and win ribbons.'' He shrugged.
''So we took the biscuits home.''

''Did you eat them?'' she persisted.

He shook his head and he shuddered again.

''Then what did you do with them?'' she asked, thinking
he probably fed them to the cattle dogs or some livestock.

''Well, actually, we took them out to the skeet field and
used them for clay pigeons,'' he confessed with a grin.
''They were the best damned targets we ever had, but we
didn't dare say where we got them!''

She put her face in her hands and burst out laughing.
''Oh, the poor girl!'' she chuckled.

''Don't worry, we'd never tell her,'' he promised. ''But
we did ask her for another pan of biscuits, without telling
her why.'' He sighed. ''That woman has a ready-made profession as a target maker, and we haven't got the guts to
tell her so. Hell of a shame!''

She brushed at her eyes with the hem of her blouse. Poor
Janie. And she'd been jealous.

''What does she look like?'' she asked, curious.

''She comes up to my shoulder. She's got light brown
hair, longer than yours, and her eyes are green. If she didn't
know everything, and tell you so every time you saw her,
she might get married one day.''

''You don't want to marry her?'' she teased. ''Not even
for an inexhaustible supply of skeet targets?''

''I don't want to marry anybody,'' he said bluntly, and
he looked her straight in the eye when he said it. ''I love
my freedom.''

She sighed and smiled. ''So do I,'' she confessed. ''I
don't think I could ever settle for diapers and dishes. Not
with my background.''

''You were a science major, weren't you?'' he asked
abruptly.

''Yes. Chemistry and biology, genetics—stuff like that.
I made good grades, but it was hard work. Then I went

right to work for my boss, straight out of college. I need to be two people, just to catch up. I run my legs off. The stress is pretty bad sometimes.''

"No wonder keeping house and baking biscuits seemed like a holiday to you," he said to himself.

"It's been fun," she agreed. "I love to cook. I do it a lot, at home. I used to when Mama was alive," she recalled. "She hated housework and cooking. I came home from work and did it all."

"I've read about the sort of work you do," he commented, recalling articles he'd seen in the daily newspaper. "You're second only to a physician in authority. The only thing you can't do is write a prescription without his supervision."

"That's true." She smiled.

He studied her slender body, her exquisite figure nicely outlined by the garments she was wearing. "All those years, nothing but textbooks and exams and, then, a hectic career. No men?" he added, with a calculating stare.

"I dated," she replied. "I just couldn't afford to get serious about anybody. My father scraped and begged and borrowed to get the money to finance my nursing education," she told him. "Even Mike…contributed to it." She drew in a steadying breath and locked her fingers together on her lap. "It would have been so petty of me to throw all that up, just so I could go to parties and get drunk with the other students."

"Surely there wasn't much of that, at a community college?"

She laughed. "You'd be surprised. There was all too much, for my taste. But I didn't live on campus. I lived at home and commuted." She met his searching gaze. "That party I was at, when Leo was attacked—the woman who gave it was a college classmate who works for a doctor in our practice. I knew she sort of had a reputation. I guess I should have realized how wild things would get, but I was so depressed that I let her pressure me into going to the party. It was a mistake.''

''A lucky mistake, for my brother,'' Rey said gently. ''He might have been killed, if you hadn't come along when you did.'' He scowled. ''You said, you ran at the attackers, waving your arms.''

She nodded. ''Mike taught me about shock tactics,'' she said sadly. ''I was afraid it wouldn't work, but I had no weapon, no other way of stopping them. So I took the risk.''

''I'm grateful that you did.'' He shook his head slowly. ''But it was an act of lunacy, Meredith. You could have been lying on the grass next to Leo.''

''But I wasn't.'' She hunched her shoulders as if she felt a chill. ''I think there might be a force behind every single chain of events,'' she said thoughtfully. ''I don't believe in chaos,'' she elaborated. ''The body is such a messy, beautiful miracle. A single cell has chemical processes that are so complex, so meticulously crafted, that I can't believe life is an accident. If it isn't accidental, it has to be planned.'' She shrugged. ''That's simple logic. That's why I don't think God is a myth.''

They were silent for a moment. ''You're the most intriguing woman I've ever met,'' he murmured, and his dark eyes fell to her soft, full mouth.

''Surely not?'' she asked demurely. ''I don't have any secrets left.''

''That's what you think,'' he said in a soft, low tone.

She looked up and he moved toward her, one hand catching the wooden headboard as he levered his hard mouth down against her soft one.

Her hands instinctively went to his chest, but its muscular warmth was fascinating. She'd never done anything really intimate with her infrequent dates, having been completely turned off by men with fast reputations. She preferred gentlemen to rounders. She knew that Rey had been a rounder. She wanted to draw away. She really did.

But Rey Hart was completely out of her experience. He wasn't aggressive and insistent, as one of Meredith's rare dates had been. He didn't rush at her. He didn't insist. He wasn't insulting with the speed of his advances. He simply bent and kissed her, slowly and gently, with nothing more intimate than his hard, tender lips touching hers. He nibbled her upper lip and lifted his mouth slowly.

"You're doing a surfboard imitation," he murmured. "There's no need. I'm too good a cattleman to rush my fences."

She was trying to understand the slow, sensuous speech when his lips came down on hers again and caressed her upper lip. Her hands pressed flat against his muscular chest. She liked the way he felt. She could feel the quick, strong pulse of his heart under her palms. She could feel the growing rise and fall of his breathing.

His teeth nibbled her lips again, tenderly, and she found her hands moving under his arms and around him. She wanted to be held close, tight. She wanted him to envelop her against him. She wanted something more than this torturous teasing of his mouth on hers.

She made a husky, high-pitched little cry into his mouth and her nails bit into the solid muscles of his back.

"What do you want?" he whispered just above her lips.

"Kiss me," she moaned huskily.

"Kisses are dangerous, didn't you know?" he murmured, smiling against her responsive mouth. "They can be very addictive."

She was following his lips mindlessly. Her body was on fire. She'd never felt such headlong desire. Belatedly she realized that his hands were at her rib cage. Whether by accident or design, they were moving slowly up and down, up and down, so that his long fingers just lightly brushed the underswell of her breasts. It was extremely provocative. It was arousing.

She caught her breath as they moved ever closer to entrapment, and her eyes locked into his.

"Don't you like it this way?" he asked at her lips, brushing his mouth against them.

"Like...it?" she murmured mindlessly. Her body was reaching up toward those tormenting hands. She was shivering with every pulsating motion of her body, trembling with new and exciting surges of pleasure.

He laughed softly, sensuously. "Never mind." He lifted a hand to her hair and tugged out the hairpins, so that her beautiful long hair fell down around her shoulders. He tugged aside the top she was wearing, so that her shoulder was bare. Then he bent to it with his mouth, and she felt the warm, moist press of his lips right in the hollow of her shoulder.

Her nails dug into him. She lifted toward his mouth with a hoarse moan as she felt the slow tracing of his tongue against skin that had never known a man's touch. She was on fire. She was going to go up in flames right here. She didn't want to think, see, hear anything. She only wanted Rey to keep on touching her, to keep on holding her, to never, never stop...!

Eight

Just when the world was spinning away in a warm, pleasurable oblivion, the sound of loud, urgent footsteps echoed down the hall and brought Rey upright.

He looked at her with narrow, blank eyes as the sound grew louder. He cursed under his breath and got to his feet, keeping his back to her as he moved to the window, gripped the curtains and stared out at the pasture beyond.

Meredith dragged the bedspread up under her arms, over her clothes, and tried to steady her breathing. When she remembered what she and Rey had been doing, she blushed.

The door, ajar, was pushed completely open, and Leo came in with a tray. On it were a china cup and saucer, with a silver coffeepot, a silver cream and sugar service and a napkin and spoon. On a china plate were some dainty little chicken salad sandwiches.

"I thought you might be hungry," Leo said with a gentle smile as he put the tray on her lap. It had legs, so it would stand alone over her lap. "Mrs. Lewis came over to fix supper, and I had her make you these."

"Thank you!" she exclaimed. "And thank Mrs. Lewis, too. I was just starting to feel empty!"

Rey made an odd sound and she reached for a tiny sandwich very quickly, not daring to glance at him after the enthusiastic and unwise remark she'd just made.

Leo turned his eyes toward his brother. "Something wrong with you?" he asked curiously.

"Stomach cramp," Rey said without turning. "I had chili and salsa for lunch. Heartburn's killing me!"

"You should go and take an antacid tablet," Leo advised. "And drink some milk."

"I guess I'd better." Rey took a long breath and turned around, feeling more normal, finally. He glanced at Meredith. "I'm glad you're okay."

"I'll be fine. Thanks for the conversation," she said, and wouldn't meet his eyes. But she smiled shyly.

He just looked at her. Suddenly his dark eyes began to burn. He studied her intently, as if something had just happened that shocked him.

"Are you all right?" she asked impulsively.

He took a slow breath. He was still staring at her, to his brother's covert amusement. With her hair around her shoulders like that, sitting up in bed, smiling at him, he felt as if his whole life had just shifted five degrees. She was uncommonly pretty with her hair down. She had a warm, kind heart. She'd put her life on the line for a total stranger. Why hadn't that occurred to him in Houston, when they first told him that she'd saved his brother from attackers?

"Leo probably owes you his life," Rey said carefully. "But it bothers me that you risked your own to save him."

"Wouldn't you have done that same thing, even for a total stranger?" she mused.

He hesitated. "Yes," he said after deliberating for a few seconds. "I suppose I would have."

"See? You have all sorts of potential as a prospective husband," she added with a wicked smile, which got wider when he reacted. "You're sexy, you're rich, you drive a nice car, and besides all that, you like animals." She began nodding her head. "Definite potential."

His high cheekbones flushed and he glared at her. "I don't want to get married."

"Don't worry about it," she said soothingly. "It's perfectly natural for a bachelor to resist matrimony. But you'll come around." She wiggled both eyebrows. "If you get me a ring, I'll let you see my collection of used chewing gum wrappers and bottle caps."

He was still glaring.

Leo chuckled. "I'd love to see your used chewing gum wrappers, Meredith," he said enthusiastically. "In fact, I may start collecting right now!"

Rey stared a hole through his brother while, inside him, something froze.

"I'll even consider marrying you," Leo added wickedly.

She laughed, not taking him seriously. "Sorry. It's Rey or nobody. My heart's set on him." She frowned. "Pity I couldn't trade you something for him," she murmured to Leo.

Rey was getting angrier by the second, and uncomfortable at the idea that Leo was trying to cut him out.

"Make me an offer," Leo told her. "But he can't cook, and he has a temper worse than a sunburned rattler. Besides that, you can't domesticate him. He wears his spurs to the dinner table."

"So do you!" Rey accused.

"I sit more daintily than you do," Leo said imperturbably.

Rey rammed his hands into the pockets of his jeans and glared at Meredith again. "You can't give people away."

"I'm not trying to give you away," Leo said calmly. "I

want to make a profit.'' He scowled suddenly and his eyes widened as he looked at his brother's boots.

Meredith was staring at them, too. She pursed her lips and exchanged a look with Leo.

Rey glared back at them belligerently. ''What?'' he demanded hotly.

Both Leo's eyebrows went up, along with both hands, palms out. ''I didn't say a word!''

''Neither did I,'' Meredith assured him.

Rey looked from one to the other and finally looked down. There, on one of his feet, was a dainty little foot sock with a tassel on it, covering the steel toe of his brown cowboy boot. He'd unknowingly picked it up under Meredith's bed while he was kissing her.

Rey jerked it off, cursed royally, shot a furious glance at Meredith and his brother, who were trying valiantly not to look at him, and stomped out.

Helpless laughter erupted from the two people left in Meredith's room, and the sound of it infuriated Rey.

Leo was obviously ready to set up shop with their recently disclosed nurse, and Rey didn't like it. Leo was the plague of housekeepers everywhere, but he was also easier on the eyes than the other brothers, and he was charming. Rey had never learned how to use charm. He always looked uncomfortable when he smiled. Especially with women like Meredith, who was painfully shy and naive. He wasn't used to such women. But what made it so much worse was the dropping sensation in his stomach that he'd experienced when he'd stared at Meredith. He hadn't had anything like that since Carlie, who made his pulse race almost as fast as Meredith did when he kissed her.

He could still taste Meredith on his mouth. She didn't know much, but she made up for her lack of knowledge with enthusiasm and curiosity. He thought about carrying the lessons much farther, about baring her to the waist. His heart began to slam into his throat as he tried to imagine

what she looked like under her blouse. He already knew
that the skin of her shoulder was warm and soft, like silk.
He remembered her husky moan when he'd kissed her
there, the way her fingers had bitten into his back like little
sharp pegs.

He'd been away from women for a long time, but he still
knew what to do with one, and his imagination was working overtime just now. Meredith had attracted him when
she was just his cook. Now that he knew about the intel-
ligent, capable woman underneath the flighty camouflage,
he was fascinated with her. She was everything a man could
wish for.

Not that she wanted him, oh, no. She'd made it plain.
But that teasing speech about marriage had unnerved him.
His freedom was like a religion. He didn't want to get
married. Of course he didn't!

But it was natural to think of Meredith with children. He
could picture her baking biscuits for him every morning
and holding a child in her arms at night while they watched
television. He could picture her playing catch with a little
boy out in back, or picking wildflowers with a little girl at
her skirts. She was kind and sweet. She'd make a wonderful
mother.

There was her job, of course. He knew something about
her profession, that it was supposed to be high pressure.
She'd be called upon to make life and death decisions, to
comfort the sick and grieving, to make herself involved in
the daily lives of her patients so that she should counsel
them on how to maintain good health. Besides all that, she
had a college degree.

Rey was college educated, too, with a degree in man-
agement and a minor in marketing. He was the mind behind
the business decisions, the coordinator of the labor pool,
and the director of marketing for the brothers' cattle co-
operative. He was good at what he did. He enjoyed con-
versations with other educated people, and he'd convinced

himself that Meredith wouldn't know Degas from Dali, Domingo from Dwight Yoakum, Hemingway from Dr. Seuss. Now he knew better, and his respect for her increased.

She'd saved Billy Joe's life at the gun club. He recalled that she must have known what to do for Leo as well, when she'd found him after he was mugged. Leo really did owe her his life. She was competent, confident, and she wasn't hard on the eyes, either. She had wonderful qualities.

But he didn't want to marry her. He wasn't sure about Leo. His eyes narrowed as he recalled the way Leo conspired with her. Leo had known all about her already. Obviously they'd been talking together since her arrival at the ranch, because Leo hadn't been a bit surprised when she rushed over to manage Billy Joe's heart attack.

Why hadn't he noticed that? Leo had called for Meredith when he was in the hospital. He was obviously fond of her. Maybe he was interested in her romantically, too. He'd been interested in Tess, before Cag had walked off with her, but Tess hadn't realized it. Or if she had, she'd ignored it. Leo wasn't hard on the eyes, either, and when it came to charm, he had his share and Rey's as well.

As he walked down to the barn to talk to one of his men, Rey had a terrible premonition that Leo had been serious when he joked about being willing to marry Meredith. Would she be desperate enough, lonely enough, frightened enough, to marry Leo and give up her job and living with her father? Her father had beaten her badly. She might be looking for a way out of the torment, and there was Leo, successful and handsome and charming, just ready to take her in and protect her.

Rey felt himself choke on dread. He couldn't imagine living in a house with Meredith if she was married to his brother. He'd rather throw himself headfirst into a cement mixer!

But, then, Leo had been teasing. Leo was always teasing. Rey forced himself to breathe normally and at least give the appearance of someone who was relaxed. Sure, it was just a joke. He didn't have to worry about the competition. There wasn't any. He pulled his hat lower over his eyes and walked on down the aisle to the man who was doctoring a heifer.

Several days later, Meredith received a huge bouquet of assorted roses from Billy Joe, now out of the hospital and back on the shooting range. She put them in water in the kitchen, along with the card, which the brothers blatantly read.

"He'd marry you," Rey drawled with pure acid in his tone as he dragged out a chair and sat down to lunch. "He's been widowed twenty years."

Meredith gave Leo a mischievous glance and fiddled with putting biscuits in a linen-lined basket. "He's not bad-looking for a man his age, and it wouldn't hurt him to have a nurse under his roof." She glanced at Rey's eloquent back. "But can he cook?"

Rey sipped coffee noisily.

"And does he slurp his coffee?" she added without missing a beat.

"That was done deliberately, to show you that I don't give a damn about manners!" Rey growled.

"All right, just don't expect me to take you to any nice restaurants while we're courting," she said easily, setting the basket of biscuits on the table.

"Lady, you aren't taking me as far as the mailbox," he said curtly.

He looked ferocious. That black temper was already kindling. Meredith studied his bent head curiously. You never knew about men. She'd seen some very mild-mannered ones come to the emergency room with wives who'd been beaten within an inch of their lives. It didn't hurt to see how far a man would go when he got mad. Especially after her experience with her father.

"You'll have to learn to scrape the mud off those enormous boots, too," she went on in a conversational tone. "And not slurp your soup. Your hair could use a good trim..."

"Damn it!"

He shot to his feet, eyes blazing in a rigid face, with a dusky flush creeping along his high cheekbones with all the warning color of a poisonous reptile.

Meredith stood her ground, watching him clench those big fists at his side.

"Rey," Leo cautioned abruptly, and started to get to his feet.

Meredith went right up to Rey, looking him in the eyes, quiet, still—waiting.

Rey was breathing through his nostrils. His jaw was clenched with fury. But intelligence won easily over bad temper. His chin raised slowly. "You're testing me," he said out of the blue. "You want to know if I'll hit you."

"It's something a woman needs to know about a man," she said very quietly. "And she needs to find it out where she can get help if she needs it." She didn't look at Leo, but Rey knew that was what she meant. She smiled gently. "No, you don't hit," she said in a soft, quizzical tone. "You do have a temper, but it's not a physical one."

He was still breathing through his nose. "If you were a man, it might be," he told her bluntly.

"But I'm not a man," she replied.

Her eyes were almost glowing with feeling. He got lost in those soft, warm, grey eyes. He hated the way he felt when he was near her. He'd been fighting it ever since he carried her up to her garage apartment after she'd fainted at the hospital. He liked the feel of her in his arms. He liked kissing her. He liked the way she picked at him and teased him. No woman had ever done that before. As his older brothers had been before they married, he was taciturn and uncommunicative most of the time. His very attitude put most women off.

It didn't put Meredith off. She wasn't afraid of his temper, either. She made him into a different person. It wasn't something he could easily explain. He felt comfortable with her, even while she was stirring him to passion. He could imagine just sitting in front of the television with her and holding hands, late at night.

The image intimidated him. He sat back down, ignoring Meredith, and started putting butter and strawberry preserves on four biscuits.

Leo gave him a measuring look. "Don't eat all the biscuits."

"I'm only getting my share. She," he jerked his thumb towards Meredith, "didn't make but eight this morning. That's one for her, four for me, and three for you."

"And why do you get four?" Leo asked belligerently.

"Because she proposed to me," he said with pure smug arrogance, and a look that made Leo's teeth snap together.

"I did not," Meredith said haughtily, sitting down across from him. "I said I was thinking of you as a marriage prospect, not that I actually wanted to go through with a ceremony." She cleared her throat. "I'll have to see how you work out."

Rey smiled faintly. "That sounds interesting."

He didn't necessarily mean what it sounded like he meant. She mustn't jump to any conclusions here. But her cheeks were getting very rosy.

He noticed that. It was a devilish game they were playing, and he could do it better. He stared pointedly at her soft mouth as he put a cube of fresh pear into his mouth, slowly and deliberately.

She felt very uncomfortable in odd places when he did that. She ate her beef and gravy and tried to ignore him.

"I like having fresh fruit," Rey said with a slow smile.

He speared a grape with his fork and eased it slowly between his lips.

She moved restlessly in her chair. "It's healthy stuff."

"No wonder you were trying to get us to eat right," Leo said, trying to break the growing spell Rey was casting on her. "You teach nutrition, I suppose."

"In a way. I'm supposed to counsel patients on changing bad habits and making lifestyle changes when they're warranted," she explained. If only her hand didn't shake while she was holding the stupid fork. Rey saw it and knew why, and she hated that damned smug smile on his lean face!

He picked up a piece of perfectly cooked asparagus spear and slowly sucked it into his mouth, using his tongue meaningfully.

"I have to fix dessert," Meredith choked, jumping to her feet so quickly that she knocked her chair winding and had to right it.

"I saw that chair jump right out and trip you, Meredith," Rey commented dryly. "You ought to hit it with a stick."

"I ought to hit *you* with a stick instead!" she raged at him, flushed and flustered and out of patience.

"Me?" Both eyebrows arched. "What did I do?"

She pictured hitting him across the jaw with the biggest frying pan she had. It was very satisfying. Pity she couldn't do it for real.

She went to the cupboard and drew out the ingredients for an instant reduced fat pudding. She had some low-fat whipped cream in the freezer that she could top it with. Meanwhile, Rey would finish his meal and stop using fruits and vegetables to torment her with. She could have kicked him.

Behind her, Rey was talking comfortably to Leo about some new equipment they were ordering, and about routine chores that had to be completed before Thanksgiving this month and the Christmas holidays next month. Most of the ranch hands would have Thanksgiving, the day after, and that weekend free. Next month, they'd have Christmas Eve and Christmas Day free, along with four days before or after, depending on the schedule. Some of the men had families in far-flung locations and they had to travel a distance for the holidays. The Harts made a practice of giving the men time off to go home during the holiday season by staggering work schedules, so that there was an adequate crew here to work when days off were assigned.

Then they moved on, naturally, to a discussion about Thanksgiving dinner.

"You're going to stay until after Thanksgiving, aren't you?" Rey asked Meredith.

She had her back to them. "Yes, I'd like to," she said, because she'd already been planning special menus and light, noncaloric desserts for it. "Unless you're planning to go away for it," she added quickly.

"The family has a Christmas party, when we all get together. We sort of save Thanksgiving for just us, so the others can have the day with their wives and kids," Leo told her. "It's been sort of hit and miss since Mrs. Lewis has been plagued with arthritis. As you know, we got her to come back to work just briefly, but her hands won't hold out to make bread and do any scrubbing with them, despite medicine. She has her children up from Corpus Christi for the holidays and cooks for them. We sort of got leftovers."

She grimaced. "Well, I'll make sure you have a big Thanksgiving dinner this year," she said gently. "With all the trimmings. Including biscuits," she added when they both looked her way.

She finished whipping the pudding, and put it in bowls in the refrigerator to chill before she sat back down. "That will make us a nice dessert tonight," she commented. "I don't suppose you want it any sooner?"

They shook their heads. "I've got a meeting with our marketing staff in half an hour," Rey said, checking his multifunction watch.

"And I've got to go over the new equipment list with our mechanic and see if we've got everything ready to order," Leo added.

"How about a nice Greek salad for supper?" Meredith asked. "I make it with Feta cheese and black olives and eggs. I bought the ingredients yesterday at the store. Except for the eggs, of course. I'll get those out of the henhouse."

"Sounds nice," Leo said with a grin.

"Watch where you put your hands," Rey murmured without looking right at her. "I haven't seen my pet snake in the barn lately."

She gave him a cold look. "If I see him, I'll get him on a stick and put him right back in the barn," she said with pure bravado.

Rey glanced at her with dancing dark eyes. "I'd pay real money to see you do that," he chided.

So would I, she thought, but she didn't say it. She just smiled smugly.

The brothers finished their last swallows of coffee and went out the door still talking business.

Later, Meredith went out to the henhouse to gather the eggs, with her straw basket on her arm. Rey had unnerved her with his comment about the damned snake. Now she was sure it was in there, waiting for a gullible victim to frighten.

She took a deep breath and walked carefully into the dim confines of the henhouse. She bit her lower lip and approached the nest slowly. She stopped dead. There was actually a snake in there. He was wrapped around the eggs. He was licking his snaky lips.

She shivered with fear, but she wasn't going to let the stupid thing make her a laughingstock twice.

She saw a long, thick stick on the straw-covered floor. She put her basket down, still watching the snake, and picked up the stick.

"It's okay, old fellow," she said to the snake. "It's okay.

I'm just going to ease you out of the nest. Don't get mad, now. I won't hurt you. It's okay.''

While she was talking, softly, she eased the stick under its coils and very carefully lifted it. It was very still, not moving its head except to hiss. So far, so good. She had it up on the stick. It was heavy.

As she pulled it out of the nest, she noticed that it was really quite long. It really didn't look much like that black and white one Rey had put in the barn. This one had a pretty brown pattern on its back and had a white underbelly. But, then, it wasn't striking at her or anything, so she wasn't worried.

She held it far out in front of her and stepped carefully out of the henhouse into the bright light. As she did, the snake hung from the stick, looking rather bored by the whole thing.

She carried it through the yard and out toward the barn. One of the men was standing by a truck, watching her progress. His jaw fell. She wondered what was wrong with him. Maybe he'd never seen a woman carry a snake around before.

"Nice day," she called to him.

He didn't answer. She shrugged and kept walking.

The barn was empty, except for the bales of hay that were stacked neatly on the bottom and the loft of the huge structure. Over against one wall there was a corn crib with stacks and stacks of dried corn, and a machine that shelled them.

"Here we go, old fellow," she told the snake. She eased him over the wooden box and slid him down into the piles of unshelled corn.

He drew back in a threatening pose and hissed at her again.

Odd, the shape of his head, she thought, frowning as she studied him. It looked like an arrowhead. That other snake's head had been rounded.

Well, it might be some other species of king snake, she supposed. Weren't there several?

She walked back out of the barn into the daylight, whistling softly to herself as she started back to the henhouse. She was so proud of herself. She'd gotten the snake on the stick all by herself, without screaming once, and she'd carried him all the way to the barn and put him in the corn crib. She wasn't afraid of the snake anymore. As Rey had said, they were beneficial. It wasn't right to kill something just because you were afraid of it, she told herself.

The man who'd been standing by the truck was nowhere in sight, but the truck was still running and the driver's door was standing wide-open. She wondered where the driver had gone. He must have been in a hurry for some reason.

Meredith went back to the henhouse, put the stick down, picked up her basket and went to gather eggs. There were no more snakes, but there were plenty of eggs. She could boil several to go in her nice Greek salad. The spinach she'd bought to make it with was crisp and cold and almost blemishless. The brothers would love a salad if it had enough eggs and cheese and dressing.

She got the last egg into the basket and walked back out again, pausing to reach down and pet one of the big red hens who came right up to her and cocked its head curiously toward her face.

"Aren't you a pretty girl?" she said, smiling. She liked the way the chicken felt. Its feathers were very smooth and silky, and the chicken made the sweetest little noises when she petted it. She'd never been around farm creatures. She found that she enjoyed the chickens and the cattle dogs and the endless cats that hung around outside begging for handouts.

Two other hens came up to her, curious about the tall creature in jeans and tank top. She petted them, too, laughing as they crowded close. But then one started to peck the eggs, and she stood up again.

She turned back toward the house, her mind on the snake and her bravery. She'd have to remember to tell Rey and Leo about it...

"Meredith!"

The loud, urgent deep voice sent her spinning around. Rey was running toward her, bare-headed, with the cowhand who'd been next to the running pickup truck at his heels.

"Hi, Rey," she said hesitantly. "What's wrong?"

He stopped just in front of her. He caught her a little roughly by the arms and took the basket away from her, setting it aside, while he looked at every inch of her bare arms and hands. He was breathing rapidly. He seemed unnaturally pale and tight-lipped.

"It didn't bite you?" he demanded.

"What?"

"The snake! It didn't bite you?" he snapped.

"No, of course not," she stammered. "I just got it on a stick, like you did, and put it in the corn crib."

"Get my Winchester," Rey told the other man in a harsh tone. "Load it and bring it back here. Hurry!"

"I don't understand," Meredith said with noticeable confusion. "What's wrong with you? Why do you need a gun?"

"Oh, baby," he whispered hoarsely. He pulled her against him and bent to kiss her in view of the whole outfit, his mouth hard and rough against hers. "Baby!"

She had no idea what was wrong, but she loved the faint tremor in his hard arms as they crushed her against his body. And she loved the way he was kissing her, as if he couldn't get enough of her mouth. He'd called her "baby..."

She held on and moaned under the crush of his lips.

He drew back. "I'm sorry. It was such a shock. I was

scared out of my wits, I didn't even stop to grab my hat when Whit came into the office…!''

Her mouth was pleasantly swollen. She looked up at him dreamily and smiled.

"You don't have a clue, do you?" he asked huskily, searching her soft grey eyes.

"Mmm. About what?" she murmured, only half hearing him.

The other man came out with a rifle. He handed it to Rey. "Safety's on," the man advised.

"Thanks, Whit."

He moved back from Meredith. "I'll go kill it."

"Kill it?" Meredith exclaimed. "You can't! It will eat the rats, it's harmless…!"

"Sweetheart," he said very gently, "you were carrying a copperhead moccasin."

"Yes?" She stared at him blankly.

"It's one of the most poisonous snakes in Texas!"

She stood looking after him with her mouth open and her heartbeat choking her. She'd been carrying the damned thing on a stick, with it hissing at her. She felt the blood leave her head. Seconds later, she was lying on the hard ground. Fortunately she missed the basket of eggs on the way down.

Nine

"**Y**ou're making a habit of this lately," Rey murmured as he carried Meredith up the stairs to the garage apartment. "I never figured you for a fainter, Meredith," he added dryly.

He was still bare-headed, but he wasn't grim now. He was smiling.

"Of course I fainted! I picked up a poisonous snake!" she gasped, still in shock.

"Well, you've got guts, woman, I'll give you that," he said with a slow smile, shifting her a little closer. "Picked up a poisonous snake with a stick and carried it all the way to the barn, and it didn't bite you. Now I've heard everything."

"It did hiss a little," she recalled, shivering.

"It had eaten three eggs," he murmured. "Probably it was too busy digesting to care where it went at the time. Lucky for you."

She laid her cheek against his broad, strong shoulder and

held on tight. She had a sudden thought. "It didn't bite you?" she asked worriedly.

"It didn't get the chance. Didn't you hear the shot? I got it as it was crawling down from the corn bin onto the floor." He chuckled. "If I hadn't gotten it, though, Bandit would have. King snakes are natural enemies of any poisonous snake. They eat them. I hate to kill even a copperhead, but we can't have poisonous snakes around the livestock, or the men. Or, especially," he added with a warm glance at her, "in the henhouse. At the very least, a bite from one can put a man in the hospital."

She shivered, and her arms tightened around Rey's neck. "I was so proud of myself," she murmured. "I had no idea I was taking my life in my hands. It didn't look exactly like the other snake, but the patterns were sort of similar. I know about snake bites because I've helped treat them, but I don't know one snake from another unless I see pictures of them!" she added defensively.

"You'll learn." He kissed her forehead with breathless tenderness. "My brave girl," he whispered. "You'll never know how scared I was when Whit came running to tell me what you were doing."

It made soft little ripples of pleasure run through her body when he said that. He was being protective about her. She closed her eyes and drank in the warm nearness of him, the easy strength of his arms as he carried her. She felt safe as she'd never felt in her whole life. It was nice to lean on somebody strong, just for a little while.

He felt the vulnerability. He told himself that he wouldn't take advantage of it, but who was he kidding? She was soft and cuddly like this, and it was almost an involuntary action when his mouth slowly moved over hers as he reached her door.

The pressure was light, comforting. She sighed under the warmth and delight of it, and her lips parted, just the least little bit.

His whole body contracted with desire at that faint response. He looked down into her half-closed, misty eyes with growing hunger.

The look was as new as the tenderness. She couldn't tear her eyes away from that dark hunger in his. She forgot the snake, the scare, the people outside in the yard, everything. He bent back to her, and she met his mouth hungrily with her own, her arms clinging fiercely to his shoulders.

He groaned aloud. It was too soon, but he didn't care. He managed to open the door and close it behind them, making a beeline for the neatly made-up bed. He barely took time to put her down on the coverlet before his body slid against and over her own, his arms under her, taking his weight while his mouth made new, insistent demands on her innocence.

He lifted his head a torturous few seconds later, and his eyes blazed into her own. One lean hand slid deliberately under the hem of her tank top. At the same time, one long, powerful leg eased between both of hers and his hard mouth began to tease around the corners of hers.

"Danger will do it every time," he murmured deeply.

"Will...do what?" she asked, burning with new longings as his hand began to move up her rib cage toward the lacy little bra she was wearing under the top.

"This." His mouth opened on hers and became quickly insistent. While he kissed her, his fingers found the catch on her bra and flicked it open. She jumped when she felt his hand on flesh that had never known a man's touch before. He lifted his head and looked into her eyes. "I know. It's new territory," he said gently. His fingers stroked the delicate, warm flesh as lightly as a breeze. "Try to think of it as a rite of passage."

She felt strange new sensations. There was a tightening, a swelling, in her breasts as he touched them. She lifted involuntarily, and her eyes mirrored her surprise.

"Innocence is a rare, rare thing these days," he said at

her lips. "I respect it. And you'd better thank your lucky stars that I do," he added as his mouth bit hungrily at hers. "Because with an experienced woman, I'd lock the door and I wouldn't hesitate a minute."

She felt the words like the caress of his hands on her body. She moaned huskily under the demanding crush of his mouth. She felt his tongue tracing her lips, teasing under them, darting and touching and withdrawing. She felt his teeth, too, in a sensual caress that only intensified the new sensations he was teaching her to feel.

She felt her back arch again as he traced around the curves of her breast without ever touching the hard, taut nipple. She wanted him to touch it. Her body ached to have him touch it. She didn't understand why it should be such a violent, aching need...!

He laughed in a soft, sexy way against her lips. "Is this what you want?"

He caught the nipple between his thumb and forefinger and she lifted off the bed with a sharp cry. Heat spread over her, through her. Her short nails dug into his back fiercely and she gasped with pleasure.

"Baby," he groaned roughly, aroused by her unexpectedly ardent response. "Baby, you turn me on so hard...!"

The top was suddenly around her collarbone and his mouth—his mouth!—was right on her nipple, suckling her while his tongue tasted the hardness with a subtle caress that made her shiver. Her hands caught in the thick strands of his dark hair and held him to her body while he explored it with his mouth. She'd never imagined that she was capable of so much passion, and so unexpectedly swift. He could do anything to her, and she didn't have the willpower to stop him. Even a simple "no" was beyond her now. She wanted more. She wanted his eyes on her, his hands on her. She wanted his body closer.

As if he knew that, both lean hands smoothed up from her waist and onto her soft breasts. His fingers were rough from hard work, but their touch was pure heaven. She caressed his nape, moving rhythmically with each slow brush of his fingers, lost in pleasure.

He lifted his head to look at what he'd uncovered. She was beautiful, not too big or too small. She was just right. He loved the way her body moved when he touched it. He loved knowing how innocent she was. He'd never been with an innocent. Making love to one was a whole new experience, with levels of pleasure he'd never tasted. Her soft little moans excited him as much as those enthusiastic fingers caressing his back.

She felt his eyes and she opened hers, looking up at him. "Am I doing it right?" she whispered breathlessly.

His body tautened even more. "Yes," he whispered. "Just right."

He bent and drew his mouth gently over hers with a soft, cherishing pressure. He felt it open under his, felt her arms pulling at him. It wasn't a good idea to let this go any farther than it already had. While he was thinking it, he was moving slowly between her long legs until his body rested in the fork of hers. He eased down against her, letting her feel the slow burgeoning of his body against her belly.

She caught her breath.

He heard it, and lifted his head. His eyes were smoldering with desire, his body was rigid with it. He was getting little surges of insistent pleasure that ran the length of his spine. Her hips moved as if they were responding helplessly to the touch of him. She was making him ache like hell.

His hand moved to her hip and bit into the soft flesh, stilling the faint motion of her hips instantly while he rested on the elbow of his other arm. "Meredith," he said softly. "That will get you seduced. Right now."

She felt hot all over. Her mind seemed barely under her control. She searched his dark eyes with wonder. Her hands were against his shirt, right on the buttons. She felt him against the lower part of her body, and it felt right. It felt wonderful. She wanted to writhe under him and tempt him into intimacy.

His hand contracted and he gave her a wise, challenging stare as he read the look on her face. "Don't do it," he said huskily. "I'm years ahead of you in experience, but I can still lose my head. You don't want me to do that. Not really."

She pulled at a stabilizing breath. Her heart was still whacking around at the walls of her chest, as if she'd been running a race. "Are you sure I don't want you to do that? I mean, if you get pregnant, I'll marry you," she said breathlessly, and with deathbed humor. "Honest!"

He looked at her as if he couldn't believe his ears. The passion drained out of him, replaced by howling amusement. He started laughing. "Damn you, that wasn't fair!" he accused.

"Well, I like that! You're laughing, and here I've made you a solemn promise," she persisted, eyes twinkling.

"Hell!" He rolled away from her and sat up on the edge of the bed to run a lean hand through his disheveled hair. He glared down at her. "Now you've got fingerprints and lipstick and perfume all over me. The men will laugh themselves sick if I go to work smelling like a flower garden."

She tugged down her top and gave him an impish grin. "We could rush into my bathroom and shower it off, together," she offered wickedly.

He laughed again. He'd never laughed as much in his life as he did with her. Was this the way she'd been, before the tragedies of the past year that had marred her life? She'd said she didn't date much, but how in the world could men ignore a sweet, pretty little woman like that?

"I can't believe you spend your weekends watching television with your father," he murmured.

"I don't. I work."

He frowned. "On the weekends?"

She sat up, reaching under her blouse to refasten the bra

he'd unsnapped. She wondered why she didn't feel embarrassed. "Seven days a week, for the past six months," she said honestly. "Before that, six days a week, and I had to rest on Sunday. I usually work ten-hour days, sometimes longer if we have an emergency."

He didn't like that. "You don't have any free time, do you?"

She shook her head. "I've been dedicated to the job since I got out of college."

"And no men," he murmured with a speculative glance.

She grimaced. "Well, there was one I liked very much. We went out together for four months, and I was very nearly in love with him. But he never touched me. I thought he was building up to it, or something." She sighed. "Then I saw him, with another man." She shrugged. "He thought of me as a friend. I thought of him as a boyfriend. I sort of lost confidence in myself after that."

"It happens, in the modern world," he replied quietly.

"Before that, I had crushes on boys who never noticed me, except to ask me to help them with math or chemistry." She searched his eyes. "Of course, I didn't exactly look like this until last year."

"How did you look?" he asked curiously.

She got off the bed, went to get her purse, and took out a plastic insert. She pulled a photo from behind a credit card and handed it to him.

His eyes widened. "Good heavens!"

She winced. "I was sixty pounds overweight, and I couldn't lose it at all. I guess I tried every diet known to man. Then I took nutrition classes and learned how to get it off the sensible way. That's why I know so much about low-fat cooking."

He looked from the photo to her face and smiled. "You were pretty before, too," he said slowly. "You know, Meredith, it's not the outside that attracts people. It's what you are, how you treat other people, that makes friends of them.

You risked your life to save my brother, then you stayed with him until his family came. I wasn't very flattering to you when we first met, but I've had a lot of time to think about what you did. You're good people. Really good people."

She flushed and cleared her throat. "Thanks." She gave him a mischievous look. "So, would you like to get married Friday, or is Monday better for you?" she added with a grin.

He chuckled. "Sorry, I have to wash my dogs."

She sighed. "Rejected again."

He pursed his lips and let his eyes run over her slowly. "You could lie back down and we could discuss it again."

"Absolutely not. I only have so much willpower. You shouldn't throw yourself at women that way unless you're asking to be seduced. It's unfair."

"You're not bad yourself, kid," he murmured with a warm smile. He got up. "I've got to go back to work. Come here."

She went to him. "Changed your mind?" she asked. "I can get a ring today…"

He put a finger over her mouth. "How do I smell?"

"Is that all you want?!" she exclaimed. "Good Lord, you got me all the way over here to *smell* you?"

He bent and kissed her hungrily, pulling her so close that she could feel him against every cell of her body. But before she could cling, he put her away. "How do I smell?" he persisted.

She sniffed him. "You smell like aftershave."

He bent and sniffed her, and frowned. "You're not wearing perfume, are you?"

She shook her head. "I'm allergic to most strong fragrances."

"You smell like flowers."

She smiled. "Herbal shampoo. Flowers don't bother me. Well, real ones do sometimes, but not flowery scent. I can use scented shampoos and wear one or two colognes, but no perfumes. They're too strong."

"At least I don't smell womanly," he said with mocking relief. "I'd never live that down."

She cocked her head and stared up at him. "There goes the shower," she sighed.

He tapped her nose. "Now, cut that out." His fingers traced the fading bruises on her cheek and jaw and his eyes narrowed. "He'll never touch you again, I swear he won't," he said in a low, dangerous tone.

Her heart lifted at the look on his face. "Oh, my, aren't we getting possessive?" she teased.

He didn't smile. "Careful," he told her quietly. "I'm not teasing."

Her eyes widened with something like wonder.

"Hasn't anyone ever stood up for you?" he asked curiously.

"Just my brother. But he never had to protect me from Daddy. I know it looks really bad, but my father was the most gentle man on earth until we lost Mama and Mike. He goes crazy when he drinks, and he never remembers what he did." Her eyes fell to his chest. She toyed with his shirt buttons, wondering absently how it would feel to smooth her fingers over his bare chest. "I miss my brother terribly," she added simply.

"I'm sure you do. And your mother."

She grimaced. "She and I weren't really very close," she confessed. She searched his eyes. "You see, what Daddy yelled about her that night you were at the house was pretty much true. She was a very attractive woman, and she had lovers." She winced. "I hated knowing that. You can't imagine what it did to Daddy. She even bragged about them."

"She doesn't sound like much of a wife," he murmured.

"She didn't act like one, either. She did love to spend money, though. That's why she picked rich lovers." Her face clouded. "I was so ashamed of her. I guess she saw herself as a modern woman. I'm not. There's a big difference between sleeping with someone you truly love, and jumping into bed with anyone who has some money."

He nodded and touched her soft, swollen mouth. "She's soured you on men, hasn't she?"

"Sort of. Until you came along, at least," she admitted, without looking at him. She stared at his shirt button. "Bad temper and all, you've got some wonderful qualities."

He gave her a wry look. "I'll have to tell my brothers. They didn't know."

She chuckled. "Thanks for letting me come here to heal, anyway."

He felt uneasy. "That sounds like goodbye, Meredith."

She sighed. Her fingers stilled on his buttons. "I can't stay much longer," she said sadly. "Even though I'd like to. My boss is shorthanded as it is, and the woman filling in for me doesn't like leaving her kids in day care. She retired when she had the second one."

"Retired?"

"Yes. She said keeping two kids in day care ate up her whole paycheck." She lifted her eyes to his. "Since her husband got a raise, it was actually cheaper for her to stay home with the kids than it was to work. She loves it."

There was a strange look on his face. He rubbed his fingertips over her short fingernails absently. "Would you want to stay home with your kids?"

She stared up at him, transfixed. "Yes, I would. Those first few years are so important. If I could find any way to do it, I would, even if I had to sacrifice some little luxuries."

"That would be tricky. You're a highly trained professional."

"One of my friends was a highly trained doctor," she replied. "She gave up her job and stayed home with her little boy until he was in kindergarten. Even then, she arranged her schedule so that she'd be there when he got home in the afternoons.''

He was frowning, and his fingers were still smoothing over hers. He wanted to ask if she thought she could get used to ranch life and snakes. He was afraid to say it. The act of commitment was still very new to him. He couldn't rush her.

He sighed, troubled. ''What does your father do, by the way?'' he asked suddenly.

''Oh, he teaches in the veterinary department of his college in Houston.''

His hand stilled on hers. ''He's a veterinarian?''

''He has a doctorate in veterinary medicine, yes. Why?''

Wheels were turning in his head. He stared at her thoughtfully. ''Will he have a job to go back to, after all the trouble he's had with the law?''

''You're very perceptive,'' she said after a minute. ''Actually, no, he won't. The college phoned before his last bender and told him not to come back. You can't blame them, either,'' she added sadly. ''What would it do to the college's image, to have an alcoholic on staff with a dangerous temper?''

''Not much,'' he had to admit. ''Did he drink before the shooting?''

''Never. Not even a beer,'' she replied. ''But he's set records in the past six months. I couldn't get him near a treatment center. At least he's in one, now.''

''Not only in it, but improving by the day,'' Rey said unexpectedly. ''He'd like you to come see him. I can run you up there Sunday, if you'd like to go.''

That was surprising. ''You've spoken to him?'' she asked.

He nodded. ''I had Leo phone Colter. He has contacts who helped arrange it.'' He drew in a deep breath. ''Your father seems pretty rational right now. Of course, he isn't drinking, either.'' His eyes darkened. ''I meant exactly what I said. He'll never touch you again in anger.''

''When he's sober, he never would. I can't believe…he really wants to see me?'' she asked haltingly.

He brushed his hand against her cheek. ''He loves you. I'm sure you love him, too. You don't throw people away because they make a mistake—even a bad one. You get help for them.''

''I tried.''

''Sure you did. But it's better this way. When he comes home, we'll decide where to go from there. For now, I'll drive you to Houston on Sunday to see him. Want to go?''

''Oh, yes,'' she said. Her expression was soft, wondering. ''You'd do that, for me?''

He smiled. ''Anything you want, kiddo,'' he murmured. ''It's the least I can do for the only woman who's ever proposed to me.''

She pursed her lips and gave him an impish look. ''We could lie down and talk about it.''

''No, we couldn't,'' he told her firmly, and chuckled as he removed her hands from his shirt. ''I have to get back to work. I was in the middle of a meeting when you did your snake charmer routine. I left twelve employees sitting in the boardroom with glasses of water and no ashtrays. At least six of them smoke, despite all the regulations. I expect they've attacked the other six with chairs by now, or vice versa. I've got to get back. Quick.''

''I'd love to go Sunday,'' she said.

''Fine. I'll run you up there Sunday afternoon. We can go to church first.''

Her eyebrows lifted. ''I'm Methodist.''

He grinned. ''So are we. It's a date.'' He opened the door. Before he went out it, he glanced back over his shoulder. ''And stay out of the henhouse for the rest of the day, will you?''

"Anything for my prospective fiancé," she said with a theatrical gesture of her arm.

He shook his head and walked out, still chuckling.

Later, she wondered what he'd meant, about making decisions when her father got out of rehab. She didn't dare think too hard about it. But it sounded very much as if he wanted to go on looking out for her.

She was a modern woman. She could look out for herself. But it was kind of nice to have a man act protective and possessive, especially one like Rey, who didn't seem the sort to do it habitually. She remembered the hunger in his lean body when he held her, when he kissed her. She remembered the strange tenderness he reserved for her. It was an adventure, just being around him. They'd known each other such a short time, really, but she felt as if she'd known him all her life. The thought of going back to Houston without him was suddenly frightening.

She did the routine things until Sunday, except that when she gathered eggs, she was overly cautious about going into the henhouse. She'd learned from Rey that snakes often traveled in pairs, so she was careful to look before she stepped anywhere that the ground was covered.

She'd become something of a legend among the Hart ranch hands already. They removed their hats when she walked by, and they spoke to her in respectful tones.

"It's really strange," she remarked at the dinner table on Saturday evening, glancing from Leo to Rey. "The men seem sort of in awe of me."

Rey chuckled and exchanged an amused look with his brother. "They are. None of them has ever picked up a copperhead on a stick."

"It let me," she reminded him.

"That's the awesome thing," Leo remarked. "You see, Meredith, copperheads have a nasty reputation for attacking without provocation. It's kind of mystic, what you did."

He pursed his lips and gave her a teasing glance over his buttered biscuit. "Any snake charmers in your family?"

"No, but Mike had a pet boa for a while, until it ate one of the neighbor's rabbits," she sighed.

"*Yuccch!*" Rey said, and shivered.

"It was an accident," Meredith insisted. "It escaped out the window and was gone for three weeks. We figured it was starving, because it hadn't been fed in so long. Besides that," she added, "the rabbit was vicious. It attacked everybody who opened the cage."

"Why did the neighbor keep rabbits?"

"He sold them for meat to a specialty grocery store."

Rey chuckled. "Maybe the boa was a reincarnated taste-tester," he mused.

Leo made a face. "I wouldn't eat a rabbit if I was starving. On the other hand, snake's not so bad. Remember when we were in Arizona on that hunting trip, camping out, and our guide caught that big, juicy rattler?"

"Sure do," Rey agreed, nodding. "Tasted just like chicken!"

Obviously that was a private joke, because the brothers looked at each other and burst out laughing.

"What became of the boa?" Leo asked, interested.

"Mike had just sold it to a breeder," she recalled sadly. "He was engaged to the sweetest, kindest girl I ever knew. It devastated her when he was killed. They had to sedate her for two days, and she couldn't even go to the funeral." She shook her head. "I felt as sorry for her as I did for Dad and me."

"What happened to her?" Leo asked.

She finished her coffee. "She became a missionary and went to South America with a group of them." She winced. "She had the worst luck...it was that plane that was mistaken for drug smugglers and shot down. I think she was one of the survivors, but she didn't come back to America with the others."

"Poor kid," Rey said.

"Colter was upset over the shooting for a long time, too," Leo recalled. "Just between you and me, he was sweet on Mike's girl, but too much a gentleman to do anything about it. He thought the sun rose and set on Mike."

"I never knew," Meredith said softly.

"Neither did Mike. Or the girl," Leo added with a smile. "Colter's a clam. He never talks."

"Is he still with the Texas Rangers?" Meredith asked.

Leo nodded. "Got promoted to lieutenant just recently. He's good at his job."

She pushed back from the table. "If you two are through, I'll just wash up. Rey's going to drive me up to see my dad tomorrow."

"What a sweet guy!" Leo exclaimed with a wide-eyed look at his brother.

"He's being nice to me, because I'm the only woman who ever proposed to him," Meredith volunteered with a wicked grin. "He feels guilty because he turned me down."

"Good. I'll marry you, Meredith," Leo volunteered at once. "You just name the time and place, and I'll buy a new suit...!"

"Shut the hell up!" Rey said curtly, and hit his brother with his Stetson.

Leo protected his shoulder. "Meredith, he's picking on me!" he wailed.

"Do you want biscuits for breakfast?" she asked Rey.

He stopped flogging his brother. "All right. But only for biscuits," Rey said. He got up and deliberately bent and kissed Meredith, right in front of Leo. "Don't stay up too late. Leo and I have to check the livestock in the barn."

"Okay. Wear a jacket," she said, smiling up at him.

He bent and brushed his mouth against hers one more time. "It's not cold."

"It is. Wear a jacket," she insisted.

He sighed and made a face, but he picked up his lightweight denim jacket from the hat stand by the back door as he went out.

Leo followed him, but with a new expression on his face. He'd seen something he hadn't expected during that teasing exchange. He wondered if Rey realized that he was in love with that sweet little biscuit-making woman. And unless he missed his guess, it was mutual.

Ten

The next morning, Meredith sat next to Rey in church and felt his hand holding hers almost all the way through the service. She felt different with him than she'd ever felt with anyone else. Rey made her feel as if she could do anything. He made her feel strong and confident and safe.

She glanced up at him while they shared a hymnal and he forgot what he was singing. They searched each other's eyes slowly, until they realized that everybody else had stopped singing and were sitting down. Smiling sheepishly, Rey sat down and tugged her down beside him.

After the service, they got amused, affectionate looks from bystanders who knew Rey and had heard about his new cook.

But he didn't seem to be the least bit embarrassed by the attention. In fact, he made a point of introducing Meredith to several people, adding the little known information that she was a licensed nurse practitioner as well as a great biscuit chef.

Meredith flushed, because it sounded as if he were very proud of her, especially when he related how her quick thinking had probably saved Billy Joe's life at the target range. Billy Joe was well-known and liked locally, so that brought even more smiles. She clung to his hand with un-ashamed delight when they left.

"See, you're already a local celebrity," he teased. "And I didn't even get around to mentioning the snake."

"We should forget the snake," she said quickly.

He chuckled. "No, we shouldn't. It wins me points if I have a...cook who isn't even afraid of poisonous snakes."

She heard that hesitation before "cook," as if he wanted to say something else instead. It made her tingle all over. She couldn't stop smiling, all the way to the Jaguar con-vertible he drove when he wasn't working.

"This is a very flashy car," she commented as he put her in on the passenger side.

"I like sports cars," he said with a grin.

"So do I," she confessed. She didn't even put on a scarf. In fact, she pulled the pins out of her hair and let it fall around her shoulders.

"Won't it tangle in the wind?" he asked when they were seat-belted in place.

"I don't care." She looked at him and smiled warmly. "I like to feel the wind."

"Me, too."

He started the car, put it in gear, and pulled out onto the highway. When they were on the interstate, heading toward Houston, he let the powerful car do its best.

"Now this is a HORSE!" he called over the roar of the wind.

She laughed with pure delight. It was the most wonderful day of her life. She even forgot where they were going in the excitement of being with him in the elegant vehicle.

But all too soon, they were pulling up at an impressive brick building with its function discreetly labeled on a metal plate near the door. It was a substance abuse rehabilitation center, three stories tall, and staffed impressively with psychologists, psychiatrists, and health professionals, including physicians.

Rey held her hand to the information desk and then up to the second floor waiting room, where her father would be brought to visit with them.

"They don't like visitors the first week," Rey explained to her. "You probably knew that," he added, remembering her profession.

"I've never had anybody in here," she said quietly. She was nervous and she looked it.

He caught her fingers in his again and held them tight. "It's going to be all right," he said firmly.

She met his eyes and took a deep breath. "Okay," she said after a minute, and her body lost some of its rigidity.

There were footsteps and muffled voices. A minute later, her father came in the door, wearing slacks and a knit shirt, and behind him was a uniformed woman with a clipboard.

"Miss Johns? I'm Gladys Bartlett," the woman introduced herself with a firm handshake. "I'm the staff psychologist on your father's case."

"Hello, Merry," her father said hesitantly. He winced when he noticed the faded bruises on her face. "I'm sorry, my dear," he choked.

Meredith let go of Rey's hand and went forward to hug her father warmly. Mr. Johns closed his eyes and hugged her back, hard. His lips trembled as he forced them together, but tears ran down his lean, pale cheeks. "I'm so sorry," he sobbed.

She patted him on the back and tears fell hotly from her own eyes. "It's okay, Daddy," she whispered brokenly, comforting him the way he'd once comforted her and Mike when they were little, and something had hurt them. He'd been a wonderful father. "It's okay," she said again. "You're going to be fine. We both are."

"My son. My boy!" He shook all over. "I said I was too busy to take her to the bank. I asked him...I *asked* Mike...to go instead. He'd be alive, but for me!"

"Now, Mr. Johns," the counselor said gently, "we've been over this several times already. You can't assume blame for the lawless acts of other people. Ninety-nine times out of a hundred, nothing would have happened if you'd asked your son to go to the bank on your behalf."

"But this was the one out of a hundred," he husked. "And I can't live with the guilt!"

"I've had my own problems with it," Meredith confessed. "I could have refused to go in to work that day and taken her instead."

"And you'd be lying dead instead of Mike," her father replied curtly. "And I'd be just as eaten up with guilt!"

"You're both missing the point," Rey said, standing up. "You can't control life. Nobody can."

They all looked at him. He stood quietly, his hands deep in his slacks pockets, and stared back. "Einstein said that God didn't play dice with the universe, and he was right. Even in seeming chaos, there's an order to things, a chain of events that leads inevitably to conclusions. People are links in the chain, but people don't control the events. Life has a pattern, even if we don't see it."

"You've studied philosophy," Mr. Johns said quietly.

Rey nodded. "Yes, I have."

The older man, with thinning hair and glasses and a faintly stooped posture, moved away from Meredith and smiled. "I took several courses in it, myself. You have a degree, haven't you?"

"I do, in business. A master's, from Harvard," Rey volunteered, something that Meredith hadn't even known.

"Mine is in medicine. Veterinary medicine. I'm..."

"I know. You're Dr. Alan Johns," Rey said, shaking

hands. "Your daughter is staying with us on the ranch in Jacobsville, baking biscuits, while she recovers."

Dr. Johns winced and flushed. "They told me what I did to you," he said, glancing shamefaced at his daughter. "I swear before God, I'll never take another drink as long as I live!"

"You won't get the chance," Rey said. "I intend to watch you like a red-tailed hawk."

"Excuse me?" Dr. Johns stammered.

Rey studied his boots. "We don't have a vet on staff. We have to call one down from Victoria, because our vets are overworked to death. It would be nice to have our own vet. We pay competitive salaries and you'd have your own house."

Dr. Johns sat down quickly. "Young man, I…!"

Rey lifted his head and stared him in the eyes. "You made a mistake. People do. That's why they put erasers on pencils. You can work for us. We'll keep you straight, and you won't have to take some sort of menial job in Houston just to make ends meet. You'll like the ranch," he added. "We have a good crew."

"Someone might know what I did," Dr. Johns stammered.

"Everybody knows already," Rey said, and shrugged. "It's no big deal to us. We've got one man who came back from cocaine addiction—let me tell you, that was a story and a half—and another one who was a habitual DWI for six years until we hired him and helped him get straight." He smiled. "We don't hold a man's past against him, as long as he's willing to stay straight and work hard."

Dr. Johns was having a hard time keeping control of himself, and it was obvious. "Young man, I'll work without a salary, if that's what it takes. And I promise, you'll never have cause to regret giving me a job."

"Not unless you keep calling me 'young man,'" Rey

said with a grin. "I'm Reynard Hart, but everybody calls me Rey."

"Glad to meet you," the older man said. "Rey."

Rey nodded. "How much longer will they keep you?" he asked, and glanced at the woman with the clipboard.

"Another week should do it," she said with a big smile. "And how nice, to see him with a settled environment to look forward to the day he leaves! I believe in minor miracles, but I don't see many. This is certainly one."

Rey gave her a complacent smile. "Miracles only happen for people who believe in them," he said, chuckling.

"Thanks, Rey," Meredith said huskily.

He only shrugged. "How could I ignore the father of the only woman who ever proposed to me?" he said, matter-of-factly, and with a smile that made her blush.

"You proposed to him?" her father asked with raised eyebrows.

"Several times," she said with mock disgust. "But he has to wash his dogs, so he can't marry me."

Dr. Johns laughed heartily.

The counselor relaxed. This was going to work out. Dr. Johns was never going to end up in rehab again, she was certain of it. She only wished she could say the same for more of her poor patients.

On the drive back to Jacobsville, Meredith was on top of the world. "Not only does he get a new job, but one doing what he always loved best, working around large animals."

"He likes cattle, does he?" Rey asked absently, enjoying Meredith's animated company.

"He grew up on a cattle ranch in Montana," she explained. "He was even in rodeo for six or seven years before he went to college."

Rey expelled a breath. This was going to work out even better than he'd dreamed. Amazing, he thought, how a single act of kindness could expand like ripples around a rock dropped into a pond.

"He's not much good on a horse anymore," she continued chattily, "but he really knows veterinary medicine."

"He might go back to teaching one day. Not in Houston," he added gently. "But Texas is a big state, and when he's been away from alcohol a couple of years, who knows?"

"The ranch will be good for him. You did mean it, didn't you?" she added quickly. "It wasn't something you said to help him want to get better?"

"I very rarely say things I don't mean, Meredith," he replied. "Well," he added with a frown, "I wasn't exactly telling the truth about washing the dogs."

"Excuses, excuses." She toyed with her purse. "Rey, thank you for giving him a second chance."

He laughed gently. "I've got an ulterior motive," he murmured dryly. "When you come to the ranch to visit him, you can make me a pan of biscuits."

"Just you? Not one to share with Leo?"

He shifted behind the wheel. "He can go find someone to make him biscuits," he said. "Surely, somewhere in Texas, there's a woman who'd do it just for him."

"Your other brothers, do their wives bake?"

"Dorie and Tess do," he said. "But Tira hasn't got a clue how to," he added on a sigh. "Simon doesn't mind. They have a cook who can. Although he's really not much on biscuits, so it doesn't matter." He grinned. "You should see him with his sons. Two of them now. They're still toddlers, and he's a whiz at fatherhood. Dorie and Corrigan have a boy and a girl and Cag and Tess have a son. That makes me an uncle five times over! Christmas is going to be a real treat this year."

She thought about Christmas. It was going to be a lonely one for her, with her father down here on the ranch.

He saw the look on her face and reached out to catch

her hand in his. "Hey," he said softly, "you're invited for Christmas, you know. We'll pack up the kids and go over to the annual Christmas party at the Doctors Coltrain. They have huge layouts of Lionel trains that they run every year, especially with a little boy of their own who'll be big enough to play with them in a couple of years. Draws a big crowd. Do you like train sets?"

She smiled. "I do." It lifted her heart to know that she was going to be included in the family get-together. She loved children. It would make the season less traumatic for her and her father, because they were missing two members of their immediate family.

"We'll make it a happy Christmas," he said softly.

She tangled her fingers into his. "I'll have that to look forward to, when I go back."

"It's premature right now, but if you decide to move down here, too, I'd bet good money that Micah Steele would offer you work."

She looked at his big, warm hand holding hers. "I like Jacobsville."

His fingers grew possessive. "I like *you.*"

"Thanks. I like you, too, and if you'll loan me your cell phone, I'll call the minister right now and we can set a date," she added with wicked haste.

He chuckled. "Hold on, tiger, I may have been lying about washing the dogs, but marriage is a big step. You have to look out for me. I know you can tame snakes and handle heart attacks, and you bake good biscuits. But how do you look in a suit, and can you dance?"

"I look great in a suit," she said firmly, "and I can do Latin dances."

He grimaced. "I can't. How about a nice, slow two-step?"

"I can do that, too!"

He glanced at her. "What do you like to read?" he asked.

The next few minutes were spent in gleeful harmony, going over things they had in common. They liked the same basic forms of relaxation, and they even thought alike on politics and child-raising. It was a very good start. Meredith had seen far too many relationships start out with nothing more than sex for a foundation, and they didn't last. It took common interests, common beliefs, friendship, to make a lasting marriage.

Marriage. That word, once so warily approached, now seemed as natural as letting Rey hold her hand all the way back to Jacobsville. She wondered where they were going together in the future, and hoped it was someplace nice.

She had to go back to work the following week. Friday morning she had her suitcase packed. She was wearing her tailored beige suit with her blond hair in a neat ponytail when she followed Rey out the front door. He carried her suitcase to his car and put it in the trunk.

"I'll be back late this afternoon," he told Leo. "If you need me, I'll be on my cell phone." He patted the cell phone carrier on his belt.

"Oh, I think I can cope," Leo drawled with a wink at Meredith. "Don't be a stranger, Meredith," he added. "We'll miss you. But thanks for making us all those pans of frozen biscuits!"

"It's a good thing you have a walk-in freezer, is all I can say," she mused, chuckling. "But don't forget the directions on how to cook them," she added. "They're only dough until then."

"I'll have it all down pat in no time," Leo promised. "Meanwhile," he added, rubbing his big hands together with visible delight, "there are still six biscuits left over from breakfast!"

"No use asking you to save me a couple, is there?" Rey asked on a sigh.

"Blood is thicker than water, except where biscuits are involved," Leo shot back. "Sorry."

Rey got in the car and started the engine without another word.

Meredith was quiet most of the way to Houston. She was oddly reluctant to go back to work, although she loved her job. She was going to miss Rey and Leo and Mrs. Lewis. She was even going to miss the chickens.

"You can come down anytime you want to," Rey reminded her, when he noticed that she was brooding. It had been hard, but he'd kept his hands to himself for the duration of her stay at the ranch. He was planning a frontal assault in the near future. This wasn't the time, though.

"I know." She stared out the window at the bare trees and chilly flat landscape. "Thanksgiving comes along pretty soon."

"Your father will be working for us by then. You can come and spend a few days while you're off."

"I might still be on call," she worried.

He was grim and silent himself, after she said that. The rest of the way to Houston, he had the radio on, letting it fill the cool silence.

He dropped her off at her father's house. It looked cold and unwelcoming as she unlocked the front door so that he could sit her suitcase inside.

She turned back to him, her grey eyes wide and sad as they met his dark ones. He hadn't removed his hat, and it was hard to see his face in the shadow of it.

"Well, thanks for everything," she began.

He stared down at her with a sense of loss. After their ride up to Houston to visit her father, there seemed to be a curtain between them. They'd been very close that Sunday. But he'd gotten cold feet, he admitted to himself, and he'd drawn back. He felt the threat of her in his heart and he was trying to run from it. Suddenly it was like trying to run from himself.

"You'll be here alone," he said quietly. "Make sure you keep your door locked. We haven't had any reports that they caught the guys who rolled Leo. Just in case, don't let your guard down."

"I'll be fine," she promised him.

She looked so small and vulnerable standing there. He hated leaving her.

"You wear your jacket when it's cold like this," she told him firmly, noticing that he was standing in the cold wind in just the shirtsleeves of his chambray shirt.

"And my raincoat when it's raining," he said with a mocking smile. "You wear yours, too."

She hesitated. "Well, goodbye," she said after a minute.

"You and I won't ever say goodbye, Meredith," he replied. "It's 'so long.'"

She forced a smile to her lips. "So long, then."

He was still hesitating. His face was absolutely grim.

"I know where a jeweler's is open this early," she said suddenly, with mischievous enthusiasm.

It warmed him to hear her tease, to see that wonderful smile. "Do you, really?"

She nodded. "You can even have a diamond. But it would have to be a small one."

His dark eyes twinkled. "You just hold that thought," he said gently. "One of these days we might talk about this marriage hang-up of yours. Meanwhile, I've got to…"

"If you say 'wash the dogs,'" she interrupted, "I'll slug you!"

He chuckled. "I wasn't going to say that. I've got to get back and finish my marketing strategy for the next year before we have our year-end board meeting."

"I guess that's pretty complicated."

"No more than treating diseases and plotting nutrition,"

he replied. He studied her quietly. "I'll miss you. Don't stay away too long."

"Why?" she prodded.

"You have to save me from attacks on my virtue from hordes of amorous, sex-crazed women," he said without cracking a smile. "Who knows when I might weaken and give in to one of them, and then where would we be?"

"I've got my heart set on a virgin," she informed him.

He laughed helplessly. "Sorry, honey, you missed the boat by a decade or so."

She snapped her fingers. "Damn!"

"On the other hand, I didn't," he said in a deep, soft voice, and moved closer. He framed her face in his lean hands and studied it hungrily for several seconds. "You make me ache every time I touch you," he whispered, bending. "I'll starve to death before you get back."

"Starve...?" She wasn't thinking. She was watching his long, hard mouth come closer. She held her breath until it settled, ever so softly, on her parted lips. And then she didn't think at all for several long, tempestuous seconds.

Too soon, he caught her by the arms and pushed her away. "You stop that," he muttered breathlessly. "I refuse to be seduced on the front lawn."

She was trying to catch her own breath. "No problem. There's a nice soft carpet just five steps this way," she indicated the hall.

"I'm not that kind of man," he said haughtily.

She made a face at him.

He chuckled and kissed her one last time, teasingly, before he pulled back and started toward his car. "I'll call you."

"That's what they all say!" she cried after him.

"Then you call me, honey," he said in that deep, sexy voice that made her melt. "You've got my number, even if you don't know it yet." He winked and went on to the car. He didn't look back, even as he drove away. Meredith's eyes followed the car until it was out of sight. She didn't cry until she was inside, behind the closed door.

She was back at work and going crazy in no time, overrun by people with everything from stomach viruses to the flu. She had a good immune system, and she didn't catch any of the ailments, but she missed Rey terribly.

Three days before Thanksgiving, her father telephoned her from the ranch, full of excitement about his new job. He seemed like a different person. He told her he was still going to therapy sessions, but in Jacobsville with a psychologist. He was doing much better, and he was going to make everything up to his daughter, he swore it. And wasn't she coming for Thanksgiving?

It took real nerve to tell him the truth, that she hadn't been able to get off because of the time she'd already missed. There was simply nobody available to replace her. She'd have Thanksgiving Day, but nothing more.

She'd tried to beg the time off to have a long weekend, but her boss hadn't been pleased and he refused. He wanted her on call that weekend, and she couldn't be and go to Jacobsville. The office held a huge clinic for the local immigrant population on Saturdays, as well as Sunday afternoons, and Meredith was competently bilingual in medical terms. It made her indispensable. Not that she minded. These people were desperately in need of even the most basic health care, and Meredith was a whiz at preventive medicine. She counseled them, advised them on nutrition and wellness, and tried not to let her heart break at the sight of little children with rotting teeth and poor vision and a dozen other ailments that money could have corrected easily. The disparity between the rich and the poor was never more evident than in minority communities.

But the fact was, she had one day off for Thanksgiving and no real time for herself. It was a reminder of just how pressured her job really was, and how demanding. She loved what she did, but she hated being made to feel guilty when she asked for time off—something she hadn't done since her brother's and mother's untimely deaths. Actually it had been a battle royal to get time off for bereavement leave, and the funerals, and she'd had to go right back to work the day after the burials. It had been too soon, but she'd thought work would be good medicine.

Perhaps it had been, but she was living on nerves. The weeks at the Hart ranch had given her a taste of a whole other life. It was one she recalled with joy and missed every day. Most of all, she missed Rey. Now she wouldn't even see him. Her father said that he'd ask someone to loan him a vehicle, and he'd come to have Thanksgiving with her. That cheered her up a little, but it would mean she wouldn't see Rey. It was a bad blow. She told her father that she'd make dinner, which cheered him up as well.

Thanksgiving Day came, and Meredith got up before daylight to start cooking. She was determined that she and her father were going to have the best Thanksgiving dinner she could manage. She'd bought a turkey and a small ham, and raw ingredients to make dressing and sweet potato soufflé, green beans, ambrosia, homemade rolls and cherry and pumpkin pies.

She'd just taken the last pie out of the oven when she heard a car pull up in front of the house. She didn't stop to take off her apron or run a brush through her disheveled hair. She ran to the front door and opened it, just in time to see her father and Rey come up on the porch.

"Happy Thanksgiving, Merry," her father said, and hugged her warmly.

Rey grinned. "We thought you might like company to help you eat all that food," he told her.

"I didn't make any biscuits," she said worriedly. "Just homemade rolls."

"I love rolls." He held out his arms. "Well, come on,"

he chided when she hesitated. "You can't treat a red-hot matrimonial prospect like me to the cold shoulder! You'll never get me to say 'yes' from arm's length!"

Her father coughed. "I'll just, uh, check on the turkey," he said with an impish smile and went into the kitchen.

Rey nudged Meredith back inside the house, closed the door, and kissed her to within an inch of her life. He barely stopped to breathe before he was kissing her again, enfolding her in a bearish embrace while he made up for what seemed like years of abstinence.

"You'll smother me," she complained weakly.

"Stop complaining and kiss me," he murmured against her swollen lips. He kissed her ever harder.

"I'm not…complaining!" she gasped when he finally stopped.

He bit her lower lip ardently. "I am," he groaned. "Come on, woman, ravish me!"

"Here?" she exclaimed, wide-eyed.

"Well, give your father a quarter and send him to the store for cigarettes!" he asked with comical desperation between kisses.

"Nobody here smokes," she pointed out.

"Excuses, excuses," he murmured against her lips, using her own favorite complaint. His arms tightened and he only stopped when he had to breathe. "What a long, dry spell it's been, Merry," he whispered huskily. "Come back here…"

She kissed him and kissed him with no thought of the future. It was wonderful to be held and cuddled and wanted. She thought she'd never felt so much joy in her whole life as she did here, in Rey's hard arms.

"There's that carpet you mentioned when I left here last time," he said breathlessly, indicating the floor. He wiggled both eyebrows. "We can lock your father in the kitchen and you can ravish me, right here!"

"Not on your life." She linked her arms around his neck.

"I won't ravish you until you agree to marry me," she managed unsteadily.

"Is that a proposal?" he murmured huskily.

"Sure. You can have a ring. I think there's a ten-year-old cigar around here somewhere with a band on it…"

He was still kissing her between words. "I'll phone the minister first thing tomorrow. You can have a blood test at work. I already had Micah Steele do one on me. He said he'd love to have a nurse practitioner of his very own, by the way, if you're interested. We can have a Christmas wedding in Jacobsville."

Her mind was spinning. She couldn't quite understand what he was saying. Of course, he was kissing her and she could hardly think at all. "Blood test…work for Micah…Christmas wedding?" she murmured.

"Mmm-hmm," he whispered, kissing her again. "You can get me a ring whenever you like, but I got you one already." He fumbled in his jacket pocket and pulled out a velvet-covered jeweler's box. He opened it and showed it to her. Inside was a glorious emerald solitaire, and a diamond and emerald wedding band. "If you don't like it, we can throw it in the fishpond and go buy you something else…"

"I love it!" she exclaimed, flustered by the sudden turn of events.

"Good. Here." He took out the engagement ring, pocketed the box and slid it gently onto her ring finger. "Now it's official. We're engaged. Remember what you just promised," he added with a wicked grin. "The minute your father leaves, I'll let you ravish me on the carpet!"

Eleven

"But, Rey, Daddy won't leave," she whispered. "There's a turkey in the kitchen!"

"He can take it with him," he said generously.

She laughed and hugged him very hard. "I can't believe this."

"Neither can I," he said, nuzzling his cheek against hers. His arms tightened. "Even when I was suspicious of you, I couldn't bear you out of my sight. I still can't. This past week has been endless. I thought we could cool it for a few weeks, while I got things into perspective. But the only thing I got into perspective was how lonely I was without you." He lifted his head and looked down into her wide, rapt eyes. "I love my freedom. But not as much as I love you."

"And I love you, Rey," she said huskily. "I was lonely, too. I feel as if I've known you for centuries."

"Same here," he replied. "We're going to make a good marriage."

"A very good marriage," she agreed, and lifted her face so that he could kiss her again. He did, at length and very nicely, until her father came out of the kitchen with a turkey leg in one hand and asked if there were plans to take the dressing out of the oven before it got any blacker. Rey told him their news while Meredith took off at a dead run to rescue dinner.

Meredith worked out a two-week notice and gave up her job, to the dismay and regret of her boss, who hadn't wanted to lose her. He did see that she couldn't have a husband in Jacobsville and a job in Houston, however, and he made them a wedding present of a beautiful faceted crystal bowl.

Micah Steele offered her a job at his office, which she accepted with pleasure, on the understanding that she could work three days a week instead of six. Micah understood being a newlywed, since he and his Callie were still newlyweds as well, even with a baby on the way.

The only hitch was that all Rey's brothers got together and took over the wedding plans, to his dismay and Meredith's horror.

"It's going to be a humdinger of a wedding," Leo promised with relish, rubbing his hands together. "Cag had this great idea for entertainment."

"I don't want to hear it," Rey said firmly.

"You'll love this," Leo continued, unabashed. "He's got this great hard-rock band from Montana coming down to play their new hit record. They just had a hit single about getting married," he added with a rakish grin. "And they're having a caterer from San Antonio bring down the buffet lunch. The wedding gown is coming from one of the couture houses in Paris…"

"But you don't even know my size!" Meredith protested breathlessly.

"We looked in your dresses," he said imperturbably.

''Got your shoe size, too, and we also looked in your drawers and got the, ahem, other sizes.'' He grinned sheepishly. ''Everything is couture, and silk. Only the best for our new sister-in-law,'' he added sweepingly.

Meredith didn't know whether to laugh or scream.

''We booked you a room at a five-star hotel for your honeymoon,'' he continued, glancing at Rey. ''You still speak French, don't you?''

''French?'' Meredith gasped.

''Well, your rooms are in Nice,'' he said. ''The French Riviera. You've got a suite, overlooking the beach. Monaco is just on down the beach from there.''

Rey whistled. ''Not bad, for a rush job.''

''We try to be efficient,'' Leo said, and his eyes twinkled. ''We even ordered her a trousseau with formal gowns and casual clothes. Lots of pinks and blues and soft beige colors. We thought pastels would suit her.''

Her mouth was open. She was trying to take it all in without fainting. She was only beginning to realize that the horror stories she'd heard from Tess about weddings and the brothers were true.

''You did kidnap Dorie and tie her in a sack with ribbon and carry her home to Corrigan!'' she gasped.

''He didn't have a Christmas present,'' Leo explained patiently. ''We gave him one. Look how well it worked out!''

''You hooligans!''

''Our hearts are all in the right place,'' Leo protested. ''Besides, Dorie could bake. Which brings us to Tess, who could also bake...''

''You blackmailed Callaghan into marrying her, I heard!'' Meredith was getting her second wind now.

''He's very happy. So is Tess.''

''And poor Tira,'' she continued, unabashed. ''You arranged her wedding and she didn't even get to choose her own gown, either!''

"She was pregnant. We had to hurry, there was no time," Leo explained matter-of-factly.

"I am not pregnant!" she exclaimed, red-faced.

Leo gave Rey a quick, speculative glance. "Yet," he replied. He grinned.

"If you would just give me a little time to organize my own wedding," she began, exasperated, and thought, I'm being nibbled to death by ducks...!

Leo checked his watch. "Sorry, I'm running late. The printer is waiting for me to check the proofs."

"Of what?" she burst out.

"Oh, just the wedding invitations. We're overnighting them to the people we invited. The governor's coming, so is the lieutenant governor. The vice president wanted to come, but he has to be in Singapore..." He frowned and checked his back pocket. "There they are! I almost forgot the interview questions. Here." He handed Rey two folded sheets of paper. "You'll have time to look them over before the camera crews move in."

Meredith and Rey exchanged wide glances. "What camera crews?" she asked.

"Just a few reporters," Leo waved them away with a lean hand. "You know, CNN, Fox, the international press...got to run!"

"International press!" Meredith choked.

"We've just signed an important export deal with Japan, didn't I mention it?" Leo called back. "They love organic beef, and we've got some. I mentioned it to our public relations people and they called the news people for us. Your father's writing the statement we're giving them. He's sure got a way with words, hasn't he?"

He waved again, climbed into his truck, and sped off.

"Invitations," Meredith said haltingly. "Clothes. Honeymoons. Reporters."

"Now, now," he said, pulling her into his arms. "Just think of all the work they've saved you. You'll have nothing to do but dress and say yes, and fly off to the Riviera with your brand-new husband!''

''But, but,'' she blurted.

''I want to marry you right away,'' he added. ''You're a qualified health professional, and I have a terrible pain that you can cure in only one night.''

She got the idea, belatedly, and hit him.

He chuckled, bending to kiss her gently. ''It's no use trying to stop them,'' he said. ''Besides, they're very good at it. I used to be, too.'' He scowled. ''Somehow, it's not as much fun being on the receiving end, though.''

She just shook her head.

The wedding was beautiful, despite her misgivings. Meredith wore the most gorgeous gown she'd ever seen, with yards and yards of exquisite lace over satin, with a long veil made of the same lace and a bouquet of pure white roses. Her father gave her away, and all four of Rey's brothers were best men. Tess, Cag's wife, stood with Meredith as her matron of honor. In a very short time, the two women had become close friends.

Most of Jacobsville turned out for the affair, but Meredith had eyes only for her handsome husband, who was dressed to the hilt as well. They exchanged rings and Rey lifted the veil very slowly. He'd been romantic and gentle and teasing over the days before the wedding. But when he looked at her now, his eyes were quiet and loving and very solemn. He bent and kissed her with such tenderness that she knew she'd remember the moment for the rest of her life.

They clasped hands and ran down the aisle and out of the church together, laughing gaily as they were pelted with rice and rose petals. At the waiting limousine, Meredith turned and tossed her bouquet. Surprisingly it was caught by Janie Brewster, notorious locally for her rubber chicken dinners and trying to catch Leo Hart's eye. She blushed vividly and clutched the bouquet, her eyes on it and not on anyone nearby. Which was as well, because Leo looked suddenly homicidal as the ranch foreman elbowed him and grinned.

The newlyweds waved and dived into the limousine, already packed and ready to take them to the airport. They'd already announced that the reception would have to go on without them, to the brothers' shock and dismay.

"I hated for us to miss it," Rey told her on the way to the airport, "but I know my brothers. They'd have found some way to embarrass us."

She chuckled, snuggling close to him. "Well, we're safe now."

The flight to France was long and boring. They held hands and couldn't sleep as the little computers above the seats marked the long trail on a map, showing the progress of the flight. When the jumbo jet finally landed, they walked like zombies into the airport to go through passport control and then on to wait for their luggage so that they could get through customs and to the waiting car that would take them to their hotel. The driver, holding a sign that read Hart Newlyweds had met them at the gate and arranged to meet them at customs. Meredith was yawning visibly when they found the driver and followed him and the wheeled luggage out the door. He and Rey exchanged comments that went right over Meredith's head.

"I don't speak French," she said worriedly when they were in the car. "I took a double minor in German and Spanish."

"No Latin?" he teased.

"There's a special course of it for nursing students," she replied with a smile. "Fortunately you don't have to learn the whole language anymore, although I wouldn't have minded. I'm so tired!"

"We'll have a nice long rest when we get to the hotel."
He pulled her close. "I could use a little sleep myself!"

The car pulled up under the covered entrance and a bell-boy came out to get the luggage. Rey paid the driver and made arrangements to contact him when they were ready to go sightseeing in a day or two.

Meredith followed Rey and the luggage to the desk clerk and waited while he got the key to their suite.

It didn't take long. Rey unlocked the door and opened it. And the bellhop burst into helpless laughter.

There, on the bed, very obviously courtesy of the Hart boys, were two life-size blow-up dolls, a blond female and a dark-haired male, in the midst of a garden of thornless roses of every color known to man. They were obviously engaged in a notorious newlywed ritual.

Rey tipped the bellhop and opened the door himself, waving the man out while he tried not to bend over double laughing.

When he closed the door again, Meredith was removing the dolls and roses with tears of mirth running down her cheeks.

"Just wait until they break something, anything," she threatened. "We can have them put in body casts for a sprained ankle...!"

He came up behind her and caught her around the waist. "And I'll help you. But, later, sweetheart," he added in a soft, hungry tone as he turned her into his arms. "Much, much...later!"

She was a professional health care worker. She knew all the mechanics of marriage. In fact, she counseled young wives in them. This was totally out of her experience.

Rey undressed her with slow precision, while he kissed every soft inch of skin as he uncovered it. He never rushed. He seemed to have committed the whole night to her arousal, and he went about it like a soldier with a battle plan.

She was teased, caressed, kissed until she felt as if there wasn't a bed under her at all. The roses were scattered over the carpet by now, along with half the bed linen. She was under him and then over him as he increased the insistence of his hands and mouth on her body. She heard high-pitched little cries of pleasure and barely realized that they were coming from her own throat.

One particularly enthusiastic embrace landed them on the carpet, cushioned by the sheet and blanket and, under them, the thick comforter.

"The bed," she whispered, trembling with unsatisfied hunger.

"It will still be there when we're finished," he replied breathlessly as his mouth bent again to her taut, arching breasts. "Yes, do that again, sweetheart!" he added when she pulled his head down to her.

He guided her hands along his lean, fit body to his hips and pressed them there as he suddenly shifted between her soft legs and his mouth ground into hers with intent.

The abrupt shift in intensity took her by surprise and lessened the sharp pain of his possession of her. His hard mouth absorbed the tiny cry that pulsed out of her tight throat, and his hands moved under her hips to caress her.

After a few seconds, she began to relax. He shifted again and found the place, and the pressure, that made her lift toward him instead of trying to escape the downward rhythm of his hips.

She clung to his damp shoulders as the little bites of pleasure became great, shivering waves. She could feel him in every cell of her body, and she wanted to look at him, to see his face, but she was intent on some distant goal of pleasure that grew by the second. Her mouth opened against the hollow of his shoulder and she moaned, her eyes closed, her body following the lead of his own as the heated minutes lengthened.

Her nails suddenly stabbed into his back and she gasped.

"Yes," he groaned at her ear. "Now, baby, now, now…!"

As if her body had given him some secret signal, his hips became insistent and the rhythm increased to madness. She reached, reached…reached…until the pleasure exploded inside her and began to spread in racking hot waves from her head to her toes. She rippled with him, sobbed against his skin, as the ecstasy she'd never known flamed through her with hurricane force.

"Rey!" She cried out pitifully as the wave peaked, and she felt her body go incandescent with joy.

His hands gripped her hips as he riveted her to his insistent hips. She heard his breathing become raspy and hoarse and then stop as he groaned endlessly against her throat and his entire body convulsed over her.

She felt him shake as the madness began to drift away.

"Are you all right?" she whispered urgently.

"I'm…dying," he choked.

"Rey!"

She held him close until the harsh contractions of his body slowed and then stopped. He collapsed on her with his whole weight, his breathing as labored as his heartbeat. His mouth burrowed into her throat hungrily.

"Never like that, Mrs. Hart," he whispered huskily. "You just made me a whole man!"

"Did I, really?" she whispered with a silly giggle.

He laughed, too. "That's what it felt like." He sighed heavily and lifted his head to look at her. His hair was as damp as hers, and he looked exhausted. He brushed loose blond strands away from her cheeks. "I'm glad we waited. I hope you are."

"Yes." Filled with wonder, she touched his hard mouth, which was swollen from its long contact with hers. "I think

I swallowed the sun,'' she whispered. "It was...glorious!''
She hid her face in his throat, still shy of him, especially
now.

He laughed again, lazily brushing his mouth over her
closed eyes. "Glorious," he agreed with a long sigh. He
rolled away from her gently, onto his back, and pulled her
against him. "We fell off the bed," he remarked after a
minute.

"I thought we were thrown off it," she murmured sleepily. "You know, by the hurricane."

"Hurricane." He kissed her forehead gently. "That's
what it felt like."

"I'm sleepy. Is it normal?"

"Yes, it is, and it does worlds for my masculinity," he
drawled. "Feel free to tell anyone you like that you rav-
ished me to such an extent that I fell out of bed in my
excitement, and you went to sleep from the tidal wave of
pleasure!"

She managed one tired little chuckle. "I'll take out an
ad in a magazine," she promised. She wrapped her arms
and one leg around him, completely uninhibited now. "I
love you, but I have to go to sleep now."

"Suit yourself, but I hope you're not throwing in the
towel. I'm a brand-new bridegroom, remember, you can't
just roll over and go to sleep once you've had your way
with me...Meredith? Meredith!"

It was no use. She was sound asleep, worn-out by the
pace of the wedding and her first passion. He lay watching
her sleep, his eyes quiet and tender and loving. It had already been, he mused, one hell of a wedding night, even
if they hadn't waited for it to get dark.

When she woke up, she was wearing a nightgown and
lying on the bed, under the covers. Rey was sipping coffee
and sniffing freshly cooked food under silver lids. He

glanced up as Meredith sat up in bed and blinked her eyes sleepily.

"Supper?" she asked.

He grinned. "Supper. Come and eat something."

She pulled herself out of bed, feeling a little uncomfortable and grinning as she realized why. She sat down beside Rey, who was wearing a pair of blue silk pajama bottoms and nothing else, and looked under lids.

"Seafood," she sighed, smiling. "My favorite."

"Mine, too. Dig in, honey." He reached over and kissed her softly and gave her a wicked grin. "It's going to be a long, lovely night!"

And it was.

They came back to the ranch after several magical, wonderful days together to find the house deserted. There was a note propped up on the kitchen table, obviously left by Leo, because his name was signed to it.

"Goodbye, cruel world," it read. "Have run out of biscuits. No relief in sight. Can't go on. Have gone into Jacobsville to kidnap a cook or beg door-to-door for biscuits. If I fail, drag the river. P.S. Congratulations Meredith and Rey. Hope you liked the wedding present. Love, Leo."

"He wouldn't really kidnap a cook," Meredith said.

"Of course not," Rey agreed. But he had a very odd look on his face.

"Or beg door-to-door for a biscuit."

"Of course not," Rey repeated.

Meredith went to the telephone. "I'll call Dad."

He waited while she dialed the cottage her father occupied and tapped his foot while it rang and rang.

"Dad?" she asked suddenly. "Have you seen Leo?"

There was a pause, while Rey gestured with his hands for her to tell him something. She flapped a hand at him while she listened and nodded.

"Okay, Dad, thanks! Yes, we had a lovely honeymoon! We'll have you up for supper tomorrow. Love you, too!"

She hung up and sighed. "Well, Leo's gone to San Antonio."

"What the hell for?" he exclaimed.

"Apparently he walked out of Barbara's café with a cook in his arms and put him in the ranch truck..."

"Him?" Rey exclaimed.

"Him." She sighed. "The cook escaped out the other door and ran to get Chet Blake."

"The chief of police?" Rey looked horrified.

"Chet was laughing so hard that he didn't get to the café before Leo took off in a cloud of dust, barely escaping public disgrace. He tried to hire the little man to bake him some biscuits, but the cook refused, so Leo took harsh measures." She chuckled. "Dad said he phoned halfway to San Antonio and said he'd be back in a few days. He thinks he'll go to that genetics workshop until the heat dies down here."

"We'll never live that story down," Rey sighed, shaking his head.

"There is a solution," she remarked. "We can find him a nice wife."

He laughed even harder. "Leo's the one of us who'll have to be dragged to the altar behind a big horse," he told her. "For all that Janie Brewster is desperate to marry him, he's as elusive as smoke."

"Janie's pretty," she recalled, because the girl caught her bridal bouquet at the wedding.

"She's a doll, but she can't boil water," Rey told her. "He'd never get a biscuit if he married Janie. Besides, she's not mature enough for him."

"She could change."

"So could he, sweetheart," he drawled, pulling her close to kiss her. "But I wouldn't hold my breath in either case. Now here we are, at home, and all alone, and I'll give you one guess what I'd like you to do next,'' he whispered suggestively.

She smiled under his lips. ''Would it have something to do with flour and olive oil and skim milk and a hot oven?'' she whispered back.

He actually gasped. ''Darling!'' he exclaimed, and kissed her even harder.

She linked her arms around his neck. ''So,'' she whispered, moving closer, ''Just how badly do you want that pan of biscuits, sweetheart?'' she teased.

Chuckling, he bent and lifted her clear of the floor and turned down the hall. ''Let me show you!''

Eventually he got a pan of fresh biscuits and a whole jar of fresh apple butter to go on them—along with a nice pat of low-fat margarine. And he didn't even complain!

* * * * *

*Watch for Cord Romero's scintillating story
to unfold in July 2002 from MIRA Books*

DESPERADO

*by international bestselling author
Diana Palmer*

*Going deep undercover to crack a merciless
international child-labor ring teams Maggie
Barton up with her childhood-companion-
turned-formidable-mercenary, Cord Romero.
But the bitter taste of betrayal still hovers
between the emotionally scarred couple, both
afraid to risk their hearts despite the desire
that sizzles when they are together. Now as
they travel the globe to solve this treacherous
case, they must confront their splintered pasts
and walk a precarious tightrope between
life…and death.*

DESPERADO

*Available in a special hardcover edition in
July 2002 wherever MIRA books are sold.*

Turn the page for a sneak preview….

Chapter One

The ranch outside Houston was big and sprawling. It was surrounded by neat white fences that concealed electrical ones, to keep in the purebred Santa Gertrudis cattle that Cord Romero owned. There was also a bull, a special bull, that had been spared from a corrida in Spain by Cord's father, Mejias Romero—one of the most famous bullfighters in Spain—just before his untimely death in America. Once Cord grew up and had money of his own, he had traveled to his elderly cousin's ranch in Andalusia to get the bull and have it shipped to Texas. Cord called the old bull Hijito, little boy. The creature was still all muscle, although most of it was in his huge chest. He followed Cord around the ranch like a pet dog.

As Maggie Barton exited the cab with her suitcase, the big bull snorted and tossed his head on the other side of the fence. Maggie barely spared him a glance after she paid the driver. She'd come rushing home from Morocco in a tangle of missed planes, delays, cancellations and other obstacles that had caused her to be three days in transit. Cord, a professional mercenary and her foster brother, had been blinded. Most surprising, he'd asked for her through his friend Eb Scott. Maggie hadn't been able to get home fast enough. The delays had been agony. Perhaps, finally, Cord had realized that he cared for her...!

With her heart pounding, she pressed the doorbell on the spacious front porch with its green swing and glider and rocking chairs. There were pots of ferns and flowers everywhere.

Sharp, quick footsteps sounded on the bare wooden floors in the house and Maggie frowned as she pushed her long, wavy black hair out of her worried green eyes. Those steps didn't sound like Cord's. He had an elegance of movement in his stride that was long and effortless, masculine but gliding. This was a short, staccato step, more like a woman's. Her heart stopped. Did he have a girlfriend she didn't know about? Had she misinterpreted Eb Scott's phone call? Her confidence nosedived.

The door opened and a slight blond woman with dark eyes looked up at her. "Yes?" she asked politely.

"I came to see Cord," Maggie blurted out. Jet lag was already setting in on her. She didn't even think to give her name.

"I'm sorry, he isn't seeing people just yet. He's been in an accident."

"I know that," Maggie said impatiently. She softened the words with a smile. "Tell him it's Maggie. Please."

The other woman, who must have been all of nineteen, grimaced. "He'll kill me if I let you in! He said he didn't want to see anybody. I'm really sorry...."

Jet lag and irritability combined to break the bonds of Maggie's temper. "Listen, I've just come over a thousand miles.... Oh, the hell with it! Cord?" she yelled past the girl, who grimaced again. "Cord!"

There was a pause, then a cold, short "Let her in, June!"

June stepped aside at once. Maggie was made uneasy by the harsh note in Cord's deep voice. She left her suitcase on the porch. June gave it a curious glance before she closed the door.

Cord was standing at the fireplace in the spacious living room. Just the sight of him fed Maggie's heart. He was tall and lean, powerfully built for all his slimness, a tiger of a man who feared nothing in this world. He made his living as a professional soldier, and he had few peers. He was handsome, with light olive skin and jet-black hair with a slight wave. His eyes were large, deep set, dark brown. His eyebrows were drawn into a scowl as Maggie walked in, and except for the red wounds around his eyes and cheeks, he actually looked normal. He looked as if he could see her. Ridiculous, of course. A bomb he'd tried to defuse had gone off right in his face. Eb said he was blind.

She stared at him. This man was the love of her life. There had never been anyone but him in her heart. She was amazed that he'd never noticed, in the eighteen years their lives had been connected. Even his brief tragic marriage hadn't altered those feelings. Like him, she was widowed—but she didn't grieve for her husband the way he'd grieved for Patricia.

Her eyes fell helplessly to his wide, chiseled mouth. She remembered, oh, so well, the feel of it on hers in the darkness. It had been heaven to be held by him, kissed by him, after years of anguished longing. But very quickly the pleasure had become pain. Cord hadn't known she was innocent....

"How are you?" Maggie blurted out, hesitating just beyond the doorway, suddenly tongue-tied.

His square jaw seemed to tighten, but he smiled

coldly. "A bomb exploded in my face four days ago. How the hell do you think I am?" he drawled sarcastically.

He was anything but welcoming. So much for fantasies. He didn't need her. He didn't want her around. It was just like old times. And she'd come running. What a joke.

"It amazes me that even a bomb could faze you," she remarked with her old self-possession. She even smiled. "Mr. Cold Steel repels bullets, bombs and, especially, me!"

He didn't react. "Nice of you to stop by. And so promptly," he added.

She didn't understand the remark. He seemed to feel she'd procrastinated about visiting. "Eb Scott phoned and said you'd been hurt. He said..." She hesitated, uncertain whether or not to tell him everything Eb had said to her. She went for broke, but she laughed to camouflage her raw emotions. "He said you wanted me to come nurse you. Funny, huh?"

He didn't laugh. "Hilarious."

She felt the familiar whip of his sarcasm with pain she didn't try to hide. After all, he couldn't see it. "That's our Eb," she agreed. "A real kidder. I guess you have—what was her name?—June to take care of you," she added with forced lightness.

"That's right. I have June. She's been here since I got home." He emphasized the pronoun, for reasons of his own. He smiled deliberately. "June is all I need. She's sweet and kindhearted, and she really cares about me."

She forced a smile. "She's pretty, too."

He nodded. "Isn't she, though? Pretty, smart and

a good cook. And she's blond,'' he added in a cold, soft voice that made chills run down her spine.

She didn't have to puzzle out the remark. He was partial to blondes. His late wife, Patricia, had been a blonde. He'd loved Patricia....

She rubbed her fingers over the strap of her shoulder bag and realized with a start how tired she was. Airport after airport, dragging her suitcase, agonizing over Cord's true state of health for three long days, just trying to get home to him—and he acted as if she'd muscled her way in. Perhaps she had. Eb should have told her the truth, that Cord still didn't want her in his life, even when he was injured.

She gave him a long, anguished look and moved one shoulder restlessly. ''Well, that puts me in my place,'' she said pleasantly. ''I'm sure not blond. Nice to see you're still on your feet. But I'm sorry about your eyes,'' she added.

''What about my eyes?'' he asked curtly, scowling fiercely.

''Eb said you were blinded,'' she replied.

''Temporarily blinded,'' he corrected. ''It's not a permanent condition. I can see fairly well now, and the ophthalmologist expects a complete recovery.''

Her heart jumped. He could see? She realized then that he was watching her, not just staring into a void. It came as a shock. She hadn't been guarding her expressions. She felt uncomfortable, knowing he'd been able to glimpse the misery and worry on her face.

''No kidding? That's great news!'' she said, and forced a convincing smile. She was getting the hang of this. Her face would be permanently gleeful, like a piece of fired sculpture. She could hire it out for celebrations. This wasn't one.

"Isn't it?" he agreed, but his returned smile wasn't pleasant at all.

She shifted the strap of her bag again, feeling weak at the knees and embarrassed by her headlong rush to his side. She'd given up her new job and come running home to take care of Cord. But he didn't need her, or want her here. Now she had no job, no place to live and only her savings to get her through the time until she could find employment. She never learned.

He was barely courteous, and his expression was hostile. "Thanks for coming. I'm sorry you have to leave so soon," he added. "I'll be glad to walk you to the door."

She lifted an eyebrow, and gave him a sardonic look. "No need to give me the bum's rush," she said, falling back into her old habit of meeting sarcasm with sarcasm. "I got the message, loud and clear. I'm not welcome. Fine. I'll leave skid marks going out the door. You can have June scrub them off later."

"Everything's a joke with you," he accused coldly.

"It beats crying," she replied pleasantly. "I need my head read for coming out here in the first place. I don't know why I bothered!"

"Neither do I," he agreed with soft venom. "A day late and a dollar short, at that."

This was enigmatic, but she was too angry to question his phrasing. "You don't have to belabor the point. I'm going," she assured him. "In fact, it's just a matter of another few interviews and I can arrange things so that you'll never have to see me again."

"That would be a real pleasure," he said with a bite in his deep voice. He was still glaring at her. "I'll give a party."

He was laying it on thick. It was as if he were furious with her for some reason. Perhaps just her presence was enough to set him off. That was nothing new.

She only laughed. She'd had years to perfect her emotional camouflage. It was dangerous to give Cord an opening. He had no compunction about sticking the knife in. They were old adversaries.

"I won't expect an invitation," she told him complacently. "Ever thought of taking early retirement, while you still have a head that can be blown off?" she added.

He didn't answer. He just glared.

She shrugged and sighed. "I must be in demand somewhere," she told the room at large. "I'll have myself paged at the airport and find out."

She gave him one long, last look, certain that it would be the last time her eyes would see that handsome face. There was some old saying about divine punishment in the form of showing paradise to a victim and then tossing him back into reality. It was like that with Maggie, having known the utter delight of Cord's lovemaking only once. Despite the pain and embarrassment, and his fury afterward, she'd never been able to forget the wonder of his mouth on her body for the first time. The rejection she felt now was almost palpable, and she had to hide it.

It wasn't easy....

If you enjoyed what you just read,
then we've got an offer you can't resist!

Take 2 bestselling
love stories FREE!

Plus get a FREE surprise gift!

Clip this page and mail it to Silhouette Reader Service™

IN U.S.A.	IN CANADA
3010 Walden Ave.	P.O. Box 609
P.O. Box 1867	Fort Erie, Ontario
Buffalo, N.Y. 14240-1867	L2A 5X3

YES! Please send me 2 free Silhouette Desire® novels and my free surprise gift. After receiving them, if I don't wish to receive anymore, I can return the shipping statement marked cancel. If I don't cancel, I will receive 6 brand-new novels every month, before they're available in stores! In the U.S.A., bill me at the bargain price of $3.34 plus 25¢ shipping and handling per book and applicable sales tax, if any*. In Canada, bill me at the bargain price of $3.74 plus 25¢ shipping and handling per book and applicable taxes**. That's the complete price and a savings of at least 10% off the cover prices—what a great deal! I understand that accepting the 2 free books and gift places me under no obligation ever to buy any books. I can always return a shipment and cancel at any time. Even if I never buy another book from Silhouette, the 2 free books and gift are mine to keep forever.

225 SEN DFNS
326 SEN DFNT

Name	(PLEASE PRINT)	
Address	Apt.#	
City	State/Prov.	Zip/Postal Code

* Terms and prices subject to change without notice. Sales tax applicable in N.Y.
** Canadian residents will be charged applicable provincial taxes and GST.
All orders subject to approval. Offer limited to one per household and not valid to current Silhouette Desire® subscribers.
® are registered trademarks of Harlequin Enterprises Limited.

DES01   ©1998 Harlequin Enterprises Limited

☑ Silhouette® Desire

presents

DYNASTIES: THE CONNELLYS

A brand-new miniseries about the Connellys of Chicago,
a wealthy, powerful American family tied by blood to the
royal family of the island kingdom of Altaria.
They're wealthy, powerful and rocked by
scandal, betrayal…and passion!

Look for a whole year of glamorous and
utterly romantic tales in 2002:

☑ Silhouette®

Where love comes alive™

COMING NEXT MONTH

#1435 HIS MAJESTY, M.D.—Leanne Banks
Man of the Month/The Royal Dumonts
Prince Nicholas Dumont was annoyed when his mother sent yet another
eligible bachelorette his way. But heiress Tara York was different from
other women—she didn't want to get married. Nicholas proposed a pretend
engagement in order to satisfy their parents. But what started out as make-
believe quickly turned into undeniable passion…. Might marrying Tara
provide the perfect remedy for the restlessness of the royal M.D.?

#1436 PLAIN JANE & DOCTOR DAD—Kate Little
Dynasties: The Connellys
When Dr. Doug Connelly learned Maura Chambers was alone and pregnant,
he suggested a marriage of convenience. But soon Doug was falling for his
lovely bride. Somehow, the handsome doctor had to show Maura that he
could love, honor and cherish her and her baby—forever!

#1437 TAMING BLACKHAWK—Barbara McCauley
Secrets!
Rand Blackhawk had led a hard, lonely life. That changed when beautiful
Grace Sullivan sought his help. He tried to fight the primal attraction
between them, but he couldn't. Did he dare hope he'd found salvation in
Grace's loving embrace?

#1438 THE PLAYBOY MEETS HIS MATCH—Sara Orwig
Texas Cattleman's Club
Rich, sexy Jason Windover was charged with keeping Meredith Silver out
of the Texas Cattleman's Club members' hair. But he hadn't expected the
emotions that Meredith's fiery personality and saucy smile aroused in him.
He was prepared to tame a wildcat…but it seemed *she* was taming *him.*

#1439 CASSIE'S COWBOY DADDY—Kathie DeNosky
Cassie Wellington was shocked to discover her new business partner,
Logan Murdock, was not an elderly gentleman. In fact, Logan was a
devastatingly sexy cowboy with a wall around his heart. And though he
seemed determined to keep her at arm's length, Cassie was equally
determined to get past his defenses and make a home in his embrace.

#1440 BILLIONAIRE BACHELORS: GARRETT—
Anne Marie Winston
Because of an inheritance clause, wealthy Garrett Holden was forced to
share a cottage with Ana Birch for thirty days. He didn't trust Ana, and
he vowed to have as little to do with her as possible. Soon that proved
impossible, for Garrett found himself wanting to get *much* closer to his
beautiful housemate!